Whisper *to the* River
May, 2020.

Leigh Anne Higgins

 FriesenPress

Suite 300 - 990 Fort St
Victoria, BC, V8V 3K2
Canada

www.friesenpress.com

Copyright © 2017 by Leigh Anne Higgins
First Edition — 2017

All rights reserved.

This is a work of fiction. Names, characters, places and incidents are either the product of the author's imagination or are used fictitiously. Any resemblance to actual events, locales, or persons, living or dead, is entirely coincidental.

No part of this publication may be reproduced in any form, or by any means, electronic or mechanical, including photocopying, recording, or any information browsing, storage, or retrieval system, without permission in writing from FriesenPress.

ISBN
978-1-4602-1650-7 (Hardcover)
978-1-4602-1651-4 (Paperback)
978-1-4602-1652-1 (eBook)

1. FICTION, ROMANCE, ACTION & ADVENTURE

Distributed to the trade by The Ingram Book Company

placebo 安慰剂
placebo effect
jeopardize 危及
weird
pantry 食物储藏室

Dedication

* Connect – With Miranda Esmond-White

gig n. 演唱会、临时工、鱼叉
gig gig worker v. 记过、怀合
posters for the gig
appeared all over town
courier 情报员、送快信的人
" 专递 courier service

ниже 778-325-4768

茅乃舍レストラン
Kayanoya

巨流河 Chi, Pang-Yuan
The Great flowing river
: A Memoir of China Manchuria

Rave 胡说乱语、乱骂、吼嘴
rave about 醉心地说、倾倒
rave party
rave-up 狂欢聚会
rave review 吹捧性评论

white knuckling
white knuckle landing

saggy 下垂的
To my parents, Paula and Gerald Fry
saggy   *Until we meet again*
slack n. 松散、萧条、便裤
slack adv. 马虎地 松弛地
      v. 减缓、使松弛
slack water 平潮期
slack-water 静水的
slacker 懒惰虫
slack ness 淡季

[handwritten notes in green:]
bittersweet and funny novel filled with the richness of spirit that makes a great novel.
Romantic suspense
mini Soccer Exercises   turtle dribbling

Acknowledgements

[handwritten in orange:]
You look radiant
jamboree 鼓軍大會

Thank you to my editor, Amanda Bidnall, who did such a wonderful job with her eye for detail, flow, and story. I could not have produced this without you. Thank you to the team at Friesen Press for the professional job of book and cover design. A special thanks to my friend Margaret Walter, retired librarian, who offered me a second pair of eyes for the manuscript as it changed and evolved. Thanks to my daughter Emma Higgins for helping me with the cover concept, setting up my photo shoot, and reading over the manuscript. Thanks to my daughter Kathleen Higgins, who is my biology facts go-to person and who also read the manuscript and continually told me that I could do this. Thank you to Oliver Mann for a great back-cover author photo. Thank you to my friends and colleagues at the Greater Vancouver Chapter of Romance Writers of America. I could not have joined a more fun and supportive group. I'd also like to thank family members and friends who understood when I had to stay home and write instead of going out to play. And special thanks to my husband, Ted Higgins, who told people I was a writer before I wrote a word, just because he knew it was my dream. Your belief in me often exceeds my own, and I am so lucky to have spent over half my life with you.

[handwritten in orange:]
meaningful mama, Soccer Drills for Kids
kicking & Dribbling. Dribble 運球 Shooting
goalie 守門員 goalie skills.
Ball control, stealing a ball from an opponent 爭球
offensive 進攻

[handwritten in green:]
Escape from Montesano - Works on ball control dribbling & offensive and defensive moves

Chapter 1

THE RIVER ALWAYS SPEWS OUT HER VICTIMS. THAT'S WHAT made the rumor so ridiculous. They said he'd not only murdered his wife, but somehow pushed her out of the boat in a place where the body would never come up. Jake shoved the oars toward Glenn, the young New Zealander he'd hired for the summer.

"Sorry, boss," Glenn said. "I shouldn't have mentioned it. I just thought you'd want a heads-up. Every one of us in the bar stood up for you."

"Doesn't matter. Did you do the safety check?"

"Yeah." Glenn made a hasty exit from the supply shed.

Jake turned and slammed the palm of his hand against the wall. Trying to quash rumors in Rosetown was like trying to stop a fire by throwing gasoline on it. Better to let it go and focus on the job. A sunset trip was how he advertised this particular rafting excursion: two hours on the river as the sun lowered behind the sagebrush-filled hills, turning the water to deep green and shadows.

Glenn had already started the orientation by the time Jake stepped outside. All teenagers today. *Great*. Just what he needed. They'd better behave, because he was in no mood for any crazy antics. They stood in a circle, each of them wearing an orange life jacket and holding a paddle. One blonde, pony-tailed girl acted like a jitterbug, but the others seemed calm—as calm as teenagers could be, anyway.

Jake walked over and introduced himself. They climbed onto the raft, three on each side. Glenn sat in the seat at the back with his two extra-long pilot paddles, while Jake pushed them away from the dock. They practiced their circles and figure eights for about ten minutes before Glenn turned to him and nodded. Jake hopped into his Zodiac chase boat and started the engine.

The first section of the trip was relatively easy. They paddled past clay-colored cliffs and rocky beaches. Swallows swooped over the water, and a deer wandered down a path to drink at the river's edge.

"Paddle left!" Glenn yelled, as the canyon walls narrowed and the water picked up speed. The three crew members on the left paddled hard while the three on the right eased up.

"Paddle all!" Glenn shouted.

They hit white water, and the raft started to slither like a snake. A large jutting rock appeared. "Paddle right!" One more set of rapids and then the beach, where they'd pull out.

Glenn shouted, "Get down!"—the instruction for all crew members to lower themselves to the center of the raft. Five of the rafters did as they'd been told, but Miss Blonde Ponytail extended her arms outward in what looked like an imitation of the actress from *Titanic*. The raft took a skyward leap, and she was in the water. She disappeared then bobbed back up. Jake grabbed her by the back of her life jacket and hauled her into his boat, where she flopped like a fish. *Stupid fool.* When she succeeded in pulling herself up to the middle seat, he met her eyes. "You were showing off."

She turned her face away. "Whatever."

Whisper to the River

A shadow crossed the water. He looked up. A woman stood on the overhanging bank, her sundress flapping in the wind. She had her phone up taking pictures. *Tourist.* No one around here cared about river rafts. When she lowered her phone, she grasped her curly red hair with one hand and held it back from her face. He gave her the thumbs-up to let her know that everything was all right, and she lifted a hand in acknowledgement. He gunned the engine to catch up with the raft. The teenager was now shivering, and although he was tempted to let her freeze, he handed her a blanket. "Wrap yourself up."

Glenn had pulled over onto a sandy beach, and the crew were getting out. Jake pulled the Zodiac alongside and extended his hand to the teenager. Her friends gathered round, asking questions and treating her like a hero. *City kids.* No respect for the river. Jake and Glenn loaded the two boats onto the trailer. They all got into the van that would take them back to the launching site.

Jake started the engine and asked, "Good trip?"

"Great. Awesome. Cool," they chorused. Even Miss Show-off was smiling.

"Then you'll have to come back and do it again next year." Business was business.

Chapter 2

IN THE BRIEF MOMENT BETWEEN SLEEP AND CONSCIOUSNESS, Maggie Jackson thought she was back in her Vancouver apartment. Instead, she found herself staring at the ceiling of a motel room.

When she'd arrived, the man in the office had been listening to an organ concerto on a CD player. "Sorry for my vampire music," he'd said as he lowered the volume. "Now what can I do for you?"

"Would it be possible to stay for a few months?"

He'd looked surprised. "Yes, I suppose we could work out something. How long exactly?"

Maggie had taken a deep breath in. Time to commit. "Four months."

And that was that. Maggie had her hideout.

What was she supposed to do now? Stare at the walls? She showered, dressed, ate some toast and marmalade, and headed out the door. Yes, she was going to drive aimlessly around the town, but it beat staring at the walls of her motel unit. It *really* beat staring at the walls of a jail cell. The Ponderosa Motel was located on the outskirts of Rosetown—far enough away for free-range cows to graze under the vacancy sign.

She turned the key and the car sputtered to life. The station wagon, with its torn upholstery and lack of air conditioning, was a far cry from Carlo's Ferrari, but she couldn't complain. Not when she was free. She turned onto Ponderosa Drive, slowed to cross a cattle guard, and followed the curvy gravel road down the hill.

The downtown core consisted of about six square blocks. She passed Maynard's Restaurant, Trudy's Hair Salon, and Sam's Hardware. *A town of pragmatists.* If she ever owned a restaurant, she'd call it Sprigs—definitely not Maggie's. At a small park next to a white clapboard museum, she followed the river south. The road eventually turned to gravel, and a faded sign announced her entry to the Tilli'q'uet First Nation.

After passing a general store advertising tax-free cigarettes, she pulled over to admire a quaint yellow church standing on the edge of a bluff, its white steeple cross standing out against the backdrop of green hills. The sign to the left of the door said *Eagles Community Church. Formerly St. Michael's Anglican. Founded 1875.* She got out of the car and walked over to the bluff. The river was wider and calmer here than upstream near the motel. Spotting a wooded trail, she followed it down, stepped into the sunlight, and tripped in her cork-heeled sandals. "Damn."

A man, who stood looking out over the water, turned when he heard her. "You OK?"

She balanced herself on the slippery rocks. "Yes."

"Are you here for the service?"

She gingerly made her way over the beach. "I was just out exploring."

He extended his hand. "Mark Johnson." He had blue eyes, wire-rimmed glasses, and looked to be somewhere in his fifties. "I'm the pastor. We start at ten thirty if you'd like to join us."

How strange. She hadn't seen a single car in the parking lot. She listened for cars but couldn't hear anything except the rustle of wind in the trees. Then she tuned in to another sound—the faint hum of motors. Boats were arriving. People hopped out and greeted Mark with slaps to the back and handshakes. The children clamored toward Maggie with smiles, colorful sweatshirts, and pants tucked into gum boots.

The same man she'd seen on the river the previous night tied up, jumped out, and walked over. With his blue eyes, short brown hair, jeans, and a T-shirt that stretched over his muscular chest, he looked even better than he had in the pictures she'd taken. "Get some good photos last night?" he asked.

"I did. Was the girl OK?"

"More than OK. She was a hero when we got in."

"Wasn't that what she was after?"

He grinned, and a dimple appeared. "Exactly."

She extended her hand. "You must be Jake."

He frowned. "How did you know that?"

So defensive. She tilted her head toward the boat's logo—*Jake's River Rafting* was written in bold, blue letters across the side. Typical, but she did like the swirly white waves underneath the letters.

His shoulders relaxed and he took her hand. "Jake Jones."

"Maggie Jackson."

"What brings you to town?"

"I'm on vacation." She glanced at the trail to the church. "Actually, I'll be here until September." He raised his brows. Jeepers, she should have rehearsed her story more.

"Let's go," Mark said.

Everyone thought that she was there to join them. Jake had his head tipped to one side. Oh, heck, it wasn't like she had anything better to do today. She smiled and followed the crowd.

A banner depicting a golden eagle hung at the front of the sanctuary. As light from the high windows played over the congregation, Mark, now wearing vestments, stepped to the front and welcomed people to the church before bowing his head to pray.

Maggie closed her eyes. She felt like she'd run a marathon. Jake sat beside her, and she just wanted to snuggle up against him.

She also needed to get a grip—they'd just met.

They stood to sing a hymn, Jake a head taller than her. He held the hymn book with a strong hand, and she inched her way closer under the guise of wanting to see the book. When they sat down, he glanced her way, and she smiled. He grinned. Maybe he'd noticed that their arms now touched.

As Mark walked over to the pulpit, she remembered her father saying that a sermon should be no longer than the time it took to suck a few Lifesavers. He'd always kept a pack handy, and that had made the whole childhood church experience bearable. Mark's sermon was short and to the point, likely only three or four Lifesavers' worth.

On her way out the door, Mark took her hand. "I hope that you'll stay for lunch."

Before she could answer, Jake touched her lightly on the small of her back. "Come on. You can put some names on faces."

The congregation poured out onto a grassy area that had been set up with tables and food, and the smell of barbecued salmon filled the air. There was a festive atmosphere, like she'd walked in on some kind of celebration. Children played, adults chatted, and a few people raced back and forth from the kitchen with plates, cutlery, and napkins. She turned to Jake. "What's the occasion?"

"No occasion—just something we like to do when the weather is good."

Their eyes locked, and for a second time, she was hit with the crazy urge to snuggle up against his broad chest and feel his arms go around her. They were interrupted by the approach of a young woman with black hair and high cheek bones, her hand on the shoulder of a little girl sporting two long braids.

"Hey Jake," the woman said.

"Hey." He smiled. "Maggie, this is Lily and her daughter Rose."

"Hi," Maggie said.

Jake excused himself and walked away. *Whew.* He had a way of disconcerting her.

Lily poured a coffee. "Would you like one?"

"Sure." Maybe the caffeine would help. She hadn't really slept in weeks. It was affecting her judgment. Jake was placing a platter of fish on the table. He smiled as an older woman nudged him with an elbow. She took a sip of coffee. He really was adorable.

Mark called for everyone's attention and said the blessing. A buzz of conversation started as people loaded their plates with fish, potato salad, green salad, and pickles. Lily motioned for her to join the line. After filling their plates, they sat down, and all of a sudden, Maggie felt ravenous. She took a bite of warm bread smothered in butter and almost swooned. The barbecue salmon was melt-in-her-mouth tender. "This is delicious. Who prepared it?"

Lily looked across the table to a man with a weathered face and a barrel chest. "Dad. This is Maggie. Maggie, my dad, Ed—the cook."

"I'd love the recipe."

"First you have to catch the fish," Ed said.

Maggie laughed. "Then what? Just a minute." She pulled out a small notebook and wrote it all down, beginning with *Catch salmon.* Jake stood a distance away, and the look on his face suggested he was annoyed. Did he not like Ed? When an elderly woman named Connie joined them and invited Maggie to lunch the following Sunday, Jake's expression turned downright angry.

Beside her, Lily lowered her voice. "Jake lost his wife."

"She died?"

Lily placed a hand on her arm. "Shh. He's coming over."

He arrived, his lips turned inward, his eyes piercing. "Could I talk to you?"

Maggie rose, and he led her a little distance away.

"If you want to ask questions, you ask me," he blurted out.

She took a step back. "I'm sorry about your wife."

"Like hell you are." His eyes narrowed. "Is that why you were at the river last night? To get a visual of me, take a few pictures? Somebody tipped you off that I go to church?"

Maggie's temper flared. "It's a free world last time I checked!"

He put his hands on his hips and won the staring competition. Muscular shoulders, jaw jutted out—if she couldn't win, she could at least walk away with her dignity intact. She returned to the table, retrieved her notebook, and nodded her goodbyes. If she tried to speak, she'd cry. She didn't stop walking until she reached her car.

It wasn't until she was back at the motel that she tried to think rationally about the incident. He'd acted like she was spying on him. Was he paranoid? She pulled off her sandals, changed into her running gear, and stepped out the door. She started at a jog then increased her pace to a sprint. Why had she stopped running? Did she get too busy with work? Or was she just too busy trying to keep Carlo from exploding? Somewhere along the line, she'd stopped caring about her own health and focused only on survival.

She ran until she couldn't take another step, sinking down into the grassy meadow and looking up at the thick branches of a ponderosa pine. Tomorrow, she was going to hurt—the good kind of hurt. The kind of hurt that said she was growing stronger, not weaker. The kind of hurt that said she didn't put up with any nonsense—not from Carlo Romero, and definitely not from a disturbed and rude man like Jake Jones.

Chapter 3

"THERE MUST BE SOMETHING MORE THAT YOU CAN DO," Jake said.

Chief Constable Frank MacKenzie leaned back in his chair and looked over his reading glasses. "We've done all that we can for now."

"Frank, I've told you there's a child at stake."

"That's a social services issue."

"It's also an issue of finding out what happened to her mother!"

Frank closed the manila folder in front of him. "We can no longer make this our top priority. We searched when the trail was hot. What are we going to find now that the trail is eight months cold?"

Jake needed to calm down, use reason. "You can't just give up. Even the media knows there's another answer. There was a reporter poking around on Sunday. She actually had the gall to follow me to church."

Frank leaned forward and folded his hands on the desk. "So old McDermitt at the *Lahara Post* still thinks there's a story we're not telling him?"

Jake thought of Maggie with her straight posture and sneaky little notebook. "I don't think this reporter was from Lahara. She had that big-city feel about her."

The chief gave him a sideways glance. "You didn't make a scene, did you?"

"I took care of her."

Frank shook his head. "Jake, let me give you a few words of advice. I've dealt with the media my whole life. Love them and they go away. Antagonize them, and they'll be all over you."

It was the media that had ignited the gossip around town. He'd be damned if he'd put up with it. "I should sue the lot of them for defamation."

"Only fuels them more." Frank rose to indicate that the meeting was over.

Jake knew he was a becoming a nuisance, but he didn't know what else to do. Someday, he'd be an eighty-year-old man, hobbling into the local RCMP detachment, asking if anyone had seen his missing wife. He rose from his seat. "One more internet search on her charge cards? Maybe whoever did this has used them. Please."

Frank walked him to the door. "All right. I'll get someone onto that as soon as I can."

Maggie made her morning coffee, added cream, and stepped onto the porch in what was becoming a routine after four days in Rosetown. In Vancouver, days had passed like the snap of a finger. Here they crawled like a snail. It took her ten minutes each morning to clean her motel unit, which consisted of a bedroom, a bathroom, a small living room, and a kitchen. She'd take a walk. She'd shop. She'd come back and read. Then she'd look at the clock that hung above the kitchen cupboards and see that it was only two o'clock in the afternoon.

She wasn't allowed to contact her family. It would jeopardize their safety, and it would be traceable. Traceable! When did she have to start worrying about things like that? God, her life was a mess. Today, however, was going to be different. She'd seen a help wanted sign in the window at Maynard's Restaurant, and she was going to apply.

Dark thoughts filled her brain as she ate her Cheerios. Each time she thought about testifying, her stomach did little flip-flops. Could she really face Carlo in court?

She felt as if there were two little people sitting on her shoulders, but they weren't an angel and a devil. One was a judgmental older woman. *You betrayed the man you loved*, she said.

The second was a child with a weak, squeaky voice. *He sent you to pick up a parcel of coffee beans that just happened to have five kilograms of cocaine hidden in it. Tell me again. Who betrayed whom?* She could swear that the child's voice was growing stronger with each passing day. After all, she hadn't expected to be pulled over that day, dragged from the car, handcuffed, and thrown into a jail cell.

He couldn't help it, the older woman said. *Think of his past. Think of all that he's been through.*

Oh, he could help it, the young child piped in. *He planned for you to take the fall.*

"Shut up, both of you," Maggie said. She rinsed out her cereal bowl. She was talking to figments of her own imagination. If she didn't get this job at Maynard's, she'd be nothing more than a babbling idiot by September. Plus, her bank account had dwindled down to almost nothing. She was still paying the rent on her Vancouver apartment. She wasn't going to let that place go. She needed it for her triumphant return, when she got a new chef job in a different restaurant, preferably with a very old, dowdy boss who could never be mistaken for a romantic interest. She opened the door to a cloudy day with just a drizzle of rain and jogged across to her car.

At Maynard's Restaurant, she sat on a stool at the blue Formica counter and ordered a cup of coffee. Maynard looked to be about sixty years old. He was balding, with a white apron tied around his burly build. Tattoos adorned his arms, and his face was pockmarked, but underneath this bulldog-like appearance, Maggie recognized a decent man. As he poured the coffee, he was complaining that one of his waitresses hadn't shown up for work that day.

This was her opportunity. "I saw the help wanted sign."

"Waitressing. A few days a week. You interested?"

"I am."

He leaned on the counter. "Any experience?"

"Yes." The bells over the front door jingled. She turned to see a group of men in cowboy hats come in and take a table near the window.

Maynard straightened his back. "You're hired," he said.

It was the shortest interview of her life. "When would you like me to start?"

"How about right now?"

"Right now?" She'd planned on doing things today. Like cleaning her unit, walking aimlessly around town, and . . . Who was she kidding? She was bored to death. "Sure."

She followed Maynard through the swinging doors to the kitchen. Two old, industrial-sized refrigerators stood in one corner beside two large sinks that needed a scouring. The outdated brown linoleum floor was also in need of a mop, but the grills and pots looked immaculate. Maynard reached for a blue waitress uniform hanging from a hook on the wall and tossed it to her. "Put this on."

She put on the loose-fitting uniform and was reaching to tie her hair back when she realized that she didn't have an elastic band. She glanced at Maynard.

"Oh, don't worry about that. Just go out there and make yourself at home."

Jake entered Maynard's Restaurant and sat at a table next to the wall. He'd convinced Chief Frank MacKenzie to keep on searching, but he wouldn't be able to do it forever. At some point, he was going to have to accept the fact that Jasmine might not be found.

A woman walked out of the kitchen, interrupting his thinking. *The reporter!* He was asking himself what she was doing there when he noticed the god-awful blue waitress uniform.

She stopped in her tracks when she saw him then fled behind the counter where she waited, gripping the handle of a coffeepot. Suddenly, like she'd made a decision, she jerked the pot off the warmer and came toward him. He almost jumped out of his chair. Was she going to pour the coffee on him?

Her eyes were hazel-green with a hint of fire. "Coffee?" she asked.

"What are you doing here?" It seemed a stupid question when she was obviously working.

"As of today, I work here."

He pushed his empty coffee cup toward her. "But you were taking pictures . . . asking questions."

She poured the coffee. "What are you talking about?"

"At the river. Then at the church. You were writing things down."

"I was writing down Ed's salmon recipe and directions to Connie's house. As for the pictures, I'd never seen river rafting." She arched her brows.

Jake felt a thud of regret. He'd gotten everything wrong. "I'm sorry. I thought that you were a reporter."

She frowned. "Why would a reporter want to know about you?"

"They think there's more to the story than I've told them."

"What story?"

"My wife. She went missing. They must have told you something."

"Lily said you lost her."

"I did lose her. She went out for a walk and was never seen again."

"That's awful."

"Order up!" Maynard yelled.

She turned and walked away. By the time she returned, he was already smitten. She had a straight nose, big eyes, and a perfectly shaped chin. More than a few men had pulled off their hats when she'd gone over to take their orders.

"What would you like?" she asked.

"I'd like to take you out. Make it up to you."

She shook her head, her curly red hair stirring against her shoulders. "No thanks."

"How about river rafting?"

"*Especially* no thank you." She glanced around the restaurant to let him know she had other customers.

"Then I'll have the Denver omelet."

"Sourdough, rye, or whole wheat toast?"

"Sourdough, please. Listen, it won't be a date. Just let me show you around the town. I know some really special spots. Places you shouldn't miss. I mean, I could be your tour guide on this holiday that you're having."

She glanced out the window and back. "When did your wife go missing?"

"Eight months ago. The reporters *would not* let it rest. They hassled and hassled me. Just when I thought they'd given up, you showed up." He met her eyes. "I am sorry."

She looked like she was wavering.

"A hike? Do you like to hike?"

"I like to run." It almost sounded like a challenge.

"We can run some of it. Are you off on Friday?"

"I don't know. I just started."

He waited.

"I guess I can be off on Friday?" she finally said.

Time to seal the deal before she changed her mind. "I'll pick you up. Ten in the morning. I'll bring the lunch."

"Sure. I'm staying at the Ponderosa Motel." She glanced back at the kitchen and walked away.

Jake let out the breath he was holding in and took a sip of coffee. Some of the other guys looked his way. He smiled to himself. Up until now, he hadn't been a player, but at this moment, he felt like he'd just scored the winning goal.

Chapter 4

JAKE STROLLED ACROSS THE CENTRAL COURTYARD OF THE motel. Barbecues, picnic tables, and lawn chairs were scattered about, but the only person around was a plump woman with a load of towels in her arms. He was about to ask her for Maggie's unit number when Maggie stepped out onto a porch. She was wearing a pink tank top and denim cut-off shorts that left none of her curves to the imagination. Her hair was pulled back into a ponytail under a green baseball cap.

He jumped up the porch steps. "Ready to head out?"

"Just let me grab a water bottle."

As she disappeared back inside, he looked around. The place wasn't ramshackle, but it certainly wasn't anything to write home about. Was she going to look for another place to live, or was she really just staying until September? And if so, why?

She reappeared, carrying a small backpack. "Ready."

"I brought my dog along. I hope you don't mind."

"No problem. I love dogs."

At the truck, he pointed to his golden retriever. "This is Susie."

She glanced his way, and he could see her thinking, *What kind of man calls his dog Susie?*

As they started the drive north, she rolled down the window and rested her elbow on it. "Where exactly are we going?"

"The lookout hike. The trailhead is just a thirty-minute drive from here."

She turned to him. "Did you grow up in Rosetown?"

"I grew up north of here in a place called Beaver Lake. I moved here to start the rafting business."

"With your wife?"

"Yeah." Maggie was fishing, but he didn't want to get into the nitty-gritty of his life. *Not yet.* "For six months of the year, I run the river rafting. The rest of the time I take on electrical jobs."

"You're an electrician?"

"I am." He looked her way. "What about you?"

"I'm a chef."

Now that was something, and here she was working as a waitress. "Are you looking for that kind of work?"

"Maybe. Mostly I'm taking a break from the stress of a big restaurant."

"Something happen?"

She frowned. "Yes. I lost my job."

"Too bad."

"Not really. It was probably a good thing."

She pulled her elbow in and crossed her arms. He waited for her to go on, but it seemed to be a sore point. He drummed the top of the steering wheel. Maybe he should tell her about Jasmine. If he didn't, she'd hear the rumors, and that would be so much worse. He was just about to speak when she twisted toward the passenger-side window.

"Over there!" she shouted. A deer and her fawn were grazing on the side of the road.

Jake slowed the truck. Maggie pulled out her phone and snapped some pictures. Deer were commonplace in these parts, but Maggie looked about as excited as a kid on Christmas morning. She pulled herself onto her knees to hang her upper body out the window, exposing the back of her bare legs . . .

What was he going to say? Oh, yeah—Jasmine. He needed to tell her about Jasmine. The deer looked up, gave that silent communication to her offspring that Jake could never figure out, and the two of them darted off into the bush. Maggie plopped herself back down. She looked at him and smiled.

He was sunk. She even smelled delicious—like fruity shampoo and pastries.

He pressed his foot to the gas pedal. "Where did you grow up?"

"Calgary. My parents are still there. My older brother too. He runs a construction company."

She continued to talk about her childhood. When she told him about the time she'd sprained her ankle by jumping off the garage roof into a wading pool, he asked, "Why'd you do it?"

"Because it was there."

He laughed. "That's a mountain climber's expression."

She smiled, a beautiful wide smile. "Tell that to a six-year-old."

He told her about his sister Shelby, ten years younger, who had just graduated from high school, was a royal pain in the ass, but whom he loved to bits anyway. He talked about the logging business his father ran and his stay-at-home mother who quilted, sewed, raised chickens, and generally just fussed over all of them.

"My mother works as a clerk in a federal government office. She hates it."

Jake glanced over. "Why doesn't she quit and do something else?"

"That's what I keep telling her." She stared straight ahead. "She's got issues. She grew up with alcoholic parents, and she's terrified to do what she wants."

"Which is?"

"Be a nurse. So she nagged me to go to nursing college instead." Jake felt himself relaxing. "But you wanted to be a chef?"

She shifted in the seat to meet his eyes. "Exactly. I am a chef."

"So why *exactly* are you spending the summer in Rosetown?"

She shook her head. "I'm not telling you."

Well, that was a relief. If she could hold onto her secrets, he could hold onto his. He pulled the truck over at the trailhead and let out Susie. He grabbed his knapsack from the truck and motioned for her to go first.

She scrambled up the trail at an impressive pace, grasping at branches to pull herself over the gnarly tree roots that crisscrossed the steep incline. She stopped and examined a red currant bush then looked back at him inquiringly.

"Not ripe yet."

Susie ran up the trail and back down. Then up, then down. The dog always managed to do twice the elevation of anyone else on the hike. Maggie climbed on in silence. It felt comfortable. Lots of women had come around after Jasmine disappeared. They'd shown up with casseroles and baked goods and after a few months started asking him out for drinks or supper. He'd appreciated their concern but just wasn't interested. So why now? Why her?

At the top of the trail, they stepped out into an alpine meadow. Maggie pulled off her hat and fanned her face with it. Jake reached down and stroked Susie's head.

When they reached the lookout point, her face took on a look of pure wonder. Below them lay the town, the railway tracks, the Thompson River, and the First Nation community.

She pointed. "There's the church. It's like a postcard."

"It's my favorite place."

She turned to him. Their eyes locked, and he closed the distance. Her lips tasted like cherry lip gloss. Her tank top was moist, her body warm. She was kissing him back, standing on her tiptoes, her hands on his shoulders. He put a hand on her small waist and pulled her closer. *Damn it.* He needed to be honest. Look at what Jasmine's lies had done to him. He reached up, took her hands in his own, and pulled them down. He motioned for her to sit beside him on a nearby fallen log. Her beautiful hazel-green eyes searched his, and it took all his willpower not to kiss her again.

"Maggie, I need to tell you something."

Maggie couldn't believe her ears. Jake, suspected of homicide then cleared. Jake: another guy who just might be on the wrong side of the law. That would explain the attraction. Jeepers, they hadn't seen a single other person on the way here. She hadn't even told anybody where she was. *Calm down.* Of course he hadn't killed his wife. Did he look like a killer?

Had Carlo looked like an international drug dealer?

Shit!

She jumped up. "I told you that I liked to run."

He looked surprised. "Yeah."

"Good." She took to her heels and ran all the way back through the alpine meadow. When she looked behind her—no Jake. Susie showed her to the trail, and Maggie scrambled after the dog until she reached the truck. There she stood, trying to catch her breath. But when Susie looked up, something about the dog's sweet face caused the tears to come. Gut-wrenching tears.

She was a total idiot. Another man with another complicated history. She should have thought of it sooner. When a wife disappears, the first suspect is always the husband. Just because he'd been cleared didn't mean that he didn't do it. Carlo had seemed like a great guy at first. He'd been a successful restaurateur, romantic, generous, and most of all, mysterious. She'd slowly drawn him out, learned about his childhood tragedy and the way he'd struggled to get to where he was. Then one day she knew too much.

She rubbed the tears from her cheeks with the back of her hand. Jake would be back soon.

A man with a mystery. She couldn't do this again.

That evening, Jake stood in the laundry room, scooping kibble from a plastic container and pouring it into the bowl for Susie. After filling the dog's water dish, he snagged a beer from the fridge and twisted off the lid. Maggie had gone from panic to flight, and he'd known enough to let her go on ahead. When he'd arrived at the truck, she'd made it very clear that she didn't want to hear anything he had to say. At the motel, she'd gotten out, slammed the door, and walked toward her unit with her shoulders squared and her head erect. He'd seen the tear stains on her cheeks.

He'd blown it big-time. Next time, if there were a next time, he was going to tell her everything. Even about Cassie. He liked her enough to break the silence. If she didn't want anything to do with him after that, then so be it.

Chapter 5

MAGGIE PULLED THE PLYMOUTH INTO THE CHURCH parking lot where Lily's daughter, Rose, was playing on the grassy area with a group of children. She did not want to see Jake. On the other hand, she wasn't going to avoid him. Wasn't it enough that she was hiding from Carlo? If she ran away from every bad guy she met, she'd be running forever.

She got out and walked over to the children. "Rose, I've got something for you."

Rose looked up shyly. Maggie reached into her purse and gave her a pack of mini Lifesavers.

Lily strolled over. "What do you say?"

Rose's dark eyes sparkled. "Thank you."

Other children saw the candy and gathered round. As Maggie placed a pack of Lifesavers into each expectant hand, Mark and the people who had come by boat came up the trail from the beach.

"Maggie, nice to see you again," Mark said.

"Hi, Mark." She turned to the children. "Now remember: if Pastor Mark's sermon goes over the time it takes you to suck your Lifesavers, you get to make an official complaint. No chewing, though."

"Can I have a pack?" Lily asked with a smile.

Mark chuckled. "I'd better go make a few last-minute cuts."

Jake appeared behind the crowd. Maggie pretended she didn't see him and headed into the church. When Jake came in, he walked right past her and sat near the front. *Good.* He'd gotten the message.

Mark began his sermon, and the rustle of candy wrappers could be heard all over the sanctuary. Maggie popped a Lifesaver into her mouth and thought of her father. He'd be worried sick. Her actions had hurt a whole lot of people—especially her family. She should have known about the drugs. The clues were all there in black and white. She'd been the one to blur the whole thing into shades of gray. Funny how the human brain could click off the facts and turn on the fantasy. It was for her family's own good that they didn't know where she was. She knew them. They'd be too tempted to call, or even drive out from Calgary to see her.

On her way out the door, she was accosted by Mark. His face looked serious. "Could I talk to you in my office?"

"Am I in trouble?"

He laughed. "No, no, I just had something I wanted to ask you."

"All right. Just let me touch base with Connie. She's invited me over for lunch."

Five minutes later, Mark motioned for her to take a seat. He sat behind a desk that held a computer and piles of papers. On a bookshelf beside him, a framed picture of a pretty dark-haired woman was displayed.

He turned. "My wife, Linda. She died nine years ago."

"I'm sorry. Do you have children?"

Mark smiled. "One son. Andrew. He's attending university in Vancouver."

"What's he studying?"

"Archaeology."

"Has he done any field studies?"

"Yes, up north. He's got a passion to preserve our heritage."

Now that was interesting. Mark had blue eyes and reddish-brown hair.

Then as if reading her thoughts, he put a hand over his heart. "Yes. I'm Aboriginal."

"I wasn't sure."

"My great-grandfather was Irish." He folded his hands on the desk. "I wanted to ask a favor."

Maggie played through possibilities in her mind. Coffee server? Sunday school teacher? This was only her second Sunday. She wasn't comfortable committing to anything. "Yes?"

"Lily has applied at Maynard's, and I was wondering if you'd mind putting in a good word for her. I know she'd be a reliable employee."

Whew. "Of course. Why didn't Lily ask me herself?"

"She's too proud, but she really needs the job."

"Sure, I'll see what I can do."

He looked sheepish. "I'm sorry. I'm a meddler."

"But in a good way."

He smiled. "Thanks. How are you doing?"

Had she just invited him to meddle in her own life? For a brief moment, she felt like telling him everything, but Connie was waiting outside. "I'm well. Thanks for asking."

Mark walked her to the door. "It was nice to have you with us again. Did I meet the Lifesaver criteria?"

Maggie smiled. "I believe you did."

Jake glanced up from his coffee. Maggie strolled out of the church in a green dress that showed off a pair of long, shapely legs. She linked her arm with Connie's, and they walked over to her car. She waited as Connie eased herself into the passenger seat before walking around and getting in herself. She was patient and kind—at least to the elderly. But she sure hadn't been patient with him.

Maggie clearly had a troubled past. When he'd told her about Jasmine, she'd looked like she'd seen a ghost. He hadn't expected to see her again so soon, but she'd made it infinitely clear that she still didn't want anything to do with him. He had bigger problems to deal with anyway—like how to leave his river rafting company for three weeks. By the time he paid the extra staff to take all his shifts, he'd be operating at a loss. The lawyers he'd consulted about Cassie's custody issues had charged him two hundred dollars per hour. Sometimes he felt that circumstances were squeezing in on him until he had no air left to breathe.

On the other hand, if he had only one breath left in him, he'd use it to save Cassie from her jerk of a grandfather.

Maggie stood in a yellow kitchen, looking out at Connie's perfectly manicured backyard. White lace curtains blew in the breeze, and ornaments of pudgy birds sat on the windowsill.

"Would you like some iced tea?" Connie asked.

"I'd love some."

Connie began pulling containers out of the fridge. "It's a cold lunch. Roast beef and salads, or you could make a sandwich if you like."

"Let me help."

Connie motioned with her head. "The knives and forks are in that drawer."

When their plates were loaded, they made their way out to the front porch and sat on two padded wicker chairs. It was hard for Maggie to believe that she'd only been in this town for eight days. She felt more relaxed than she had in a long while. She took a bite of her roast beef, lettuce, and horseradish sandwich. "This is delicious."

"Thank you," Connie said.

"How long have you lived in Rosetown?"

Connie smiled. "Sixty-three years. I was a teacher when I first moved here." Her face took on a soft expression.

"From where?"

"Vancouver. I planned to come for a year, but I met my husband and never left. John's gone now. He died two years ago."

"Oh, that's too bad. Do you have children?"

"Three. All living in other towns. When I first came, I taught forty students from first to sixth grade in a one-room schoolhouse. Of course, there was the other school where John taught—the Indian residential school. Have you seen it?"

The only schools Maggie had seen were the modern elementary and high school on the outskirts of the downtown core. "No."

"It's up Carsen Drive. A big, old abandoned brick building. You should take a look." Connie shook her head as if trying to shake away a memory. "It was a terrible place."

After chatting a little more about Connie's teaching career, Maggie told her about growing up in Calgary, moving to Vancouver to attend the Vancouver School of Culinary Arts, and getting the job at La Fama. She didn't tell her much about Carlo except to say that she'd been dating the boss and had thought it best to quit her chef job when they broke up.

Connie took a sip of iced tea. "Jake seemed angry last Sunday."

"He thought I was a reporter."

"Ah, that explains it. Can't say I blame him if that's who he thought you were. Those reporters were relentless."

"Do you know him well?" *Curiosity killed the cat, and it will kill you too.* Her mother's words played in her mind, but she couldn't very well retract the question.

"He's been here for lunch."

She was in too deep. She just had to know. "With his wife?"

"No, it was always Jake alone. He'd make an excuse for her, but I think she just didn't want to come." Connie hesitated. "Maybe I'm being unfair. It's just that she'd drive around town in that little white convertible like she was avoiding everyone. I feel sorry for Jake, though. The not knowing must be so difficult."

Connie picked up their dishes, and Maggie followed her inside. She couldn't afford to feel sorry for Jake. Where had sympathy gotten her so far? In jail on her twenty-fifth birthday—that's where. She excused herself to use the bathroom.

When she came back out, Connie was loading the dishwasher. Maggie helped her wrap up the food and put it away in the fridge. Connie went to the living room and returned with a black-and-white photograph of a young woman astride a horse.

"That's you?" Maggie asked.

Connie smiled. "I rode all over these hills."

"Sounds like quite the life."

A contented look crossed Connie's face. "It really was."

Chapter 6

AS MAY GAVE WAY TO JUNE, MAYNARD'S RESTAURANT GREW busy, serving the people who traveled up the highway to holiday at the interior lakes of British Columbia. Lily had been hired to waitress, and Kyle, the sixteen-year-old dishwasher, had announced that he wanted to go to chef school when he graduated. Maynard was showing Kyle how to set the timer to make sure that the hamburgers were properly grilled.

"No lawsuits," Maynard said. "You can't poison the customer. When I worked as a logging camp cook, a bad meal was cause to get run out of camp."

Kyle flipped a burger. "Thanks for teaching me."

"*Humph.* You won't be thanking me when you're standing over a hot grill with twenty orders in front of you. You'll be wishing you chose some other way to earn your keep."

Maggie was checking the fridge for supplies. In the past few weeks, she had convinced Maynard to offer customers a salad plate on which they could add shrimp or grilled chicken, topped with fresh shredded parmesan cheese. She closed the fridge door and leaned down to remove a tray of croutons from the oven.

Maynard walked over. "What do you think you're doing?"

"Making croutons."

"That's it!" He placed his hands on his hips.

She placed the tray on the counter. "Is something wrong?"

"I'll tell you what's wrong," he said, glancing around the kitchen. "I've been stuck in this restaurant for too long, and I want to go fishing. My sales are up with those fancy salads of yours, and I'm thinking before you up and quit on me, I'd better put you in charge. Meanwhile, I'm going to catch me a trout."

Maggie relaxed. "When?"

"Next week. Three days."

"No problem."

"Kyle can come in after school and help you cook. Lily will waitress."

Leaving the croutons to cool, Maggie rinsed her hands and pushed through the swinging doors to see if Lily needed help in the front. Jake was sitting at a table near the wall, finishing off a Coke. They had put their differences aside—it was impossible to avoid him, anyway. He looked fantastic, but she'd taken the pledge: no more men with suspicious pasts.

Nevertheless, her heart skipped a beat as she went over. "How's the rafting business?"

He smiled. "Busy. Another man overboard yesterday."

"You pulled him out?"

He shook his head. "Nah. He'd already paid."

She laughed. "I guess that was a stupid question. Don't you worry about lawsuits?"

"Dead guys can't sue."

She playfully pushed his arm. *Wow.* His muscles felt like steel, and she was tempted to push on them again.

He shifted in his chair, and an energy crackled between them. "Besides, they sign a release before they set foot on a raft." He glanced over her shoulder. "Your boss is glaring at us."

Maynard stood behind the counter, his hands on his hips, his lips pursed.

"I'd better get back to work."

Maynard took a step sideways to give her room to grab some orders off the pass-through. "Why do you always talk to that guy?"

"Jake?"

"Yeah."

"He's a customer."

He scowled. "You watch out for him."

"Why?"

He glanced at the plates. "Those burgers getting cold?"

She got the message: work first. She delivered the food then turned to help Lily clear a table.

"Maynard on your case?" Lily whispered.

Maggie shrugged. "Isn't he always?"

Jake got up and walked over to the till. Maggie rang in his bill and handed him his change. For a moment, she thought that he was going to say something, but he just nodded and walked away. She was beginning to feel bad about the way she'd treated him on the hike, but even if she did want to give him a second chance, he wasn't having it.

When the lunch crowd left, the restaurant looked like a tornado had struck. Lily brought out a metal trolley with bins and a garbage bag to clear the mess.

"How old is Rose?" Maggie asked as they worked.

"Six."

She'd seen Lily's job application. She was only twenty-three. "You had her young."

Lily scraped some food off a plate. "Seventeen. Her father left town before she was born."

"He sends support, though?"

Lily turned to face her. "Ha!"

"Seriously, you could file for support."

"And let him have access to Rose?" She lifted her chin. "No thanks. We get by."

Maggie turned to unload the rack of clean mugs that Kyle had placed on the counter. She shook her head. "That must have been tough."

"It was. I dropped out of high school." Lily paused, looking like perhaps she was saying too much.

Maggie placed the last mug on the shelf and straightened her back to give Lily her full attention.

"My mother had passed away. Dad was finally sober, but not much help with a new baby. One night, I dreamt that I was in a hole. It was made of packed dirt and so deep that there was no way out, but then, over in one corner, I saw a little garden spade, and I knew I could chisel out a stairway." She smiled. "I've been climbing ever since."

"That's good."

"I've finished my GED now, and I'm saving up to move to Kamloops and take the aesthetician course. Trudy says she'll rent me a part of the salon to start my business in. We've never had an aesthetician in this town, and I know a number of women who drive all the way to Lahara for the service."

"I'd come to you for manicures and pedicures. I mean . . . if I were going to stay on in Rosetown."

"You're not?"

Here it was again. She really didn't want to lie. "No. I'm just here for the summer."

"Man trouble bring you here?"

Maggie took in a breath and slowly exhaled. "You have no idea."

"That bad?"

She met Lily's eyes. "So bad I don't even want to talk about it."

"Men. Who needs them, anyway?" Lily smiled, as if she'd just got an idea. "Hey, let's go out tonight."

"Where?"

"I'll take you to the local watering hole."

Maggie ran a cloth under the tap and wrung it dry. "Which I presume is different from the local swimming hole?"

A mischievous look crossed Lily's face. "Correct. It involves beer and dancing. I'll go home, check in, and pick you up after supper. Say eight?"

"Sounds good."

As Lily wheeled the trolley away, she turned. "By the way, I know you put in a good word for me."

Maggie continued to wipe down a table. "What makes you say that?"

Lily stopped the trolley. "Mark is the worst liar on the face of the earth. I asked him if he'd spoken to you, and he said no. But then, being a pastor, he just had to confess."

Maggie laughed.

"I don't like charity. Mark knows that. But thanks."

"It was nothing."

Lily continued into the kitchen. "I've got to get going. See you tonight."

Twenty minutes later, Maggie hung her uniform on the hook on the wall, and was about to say goodbye when she remembered Maynard's warning. She tried to appear casual as she approached him. "So what do you have against Jake Jones, anyway?"

Maynard, who'd been tying up the trash, stood up and stretched out his back. "They had a fight."

"Who?"

"Jake and his wife—the night of her disappearance. They came in here for lunch. A waitress had stood me up, so I was cooking and serving that day. They were talking in low tones. Then, all of a sudden, I heard him yell, 'That's it. I'm done.' He slammed his fist on the table, got up, and walked out. She was crying. I mean really sobbing. I went over and asked her if she was OK. She shook her head and ran out after him. I saw them get into his truck and drive away. That night she disappeared. Ain't that a coincidence?"

"Maybe she just left him."

"Nah. She drove her MG convertible everywhere. If she'd just wanted to leave, she would have taken the car. People saw them on Jake's boat that night." He paused for effect. "Jake knows the river like the back of his hand. He'd know where a body would go down and never come up."

Maggie felt a little shiver run over her back. "Is that even possible?"

"Sure."

Out of the corner of her eye, she saw Kyle shake his head almost imperceptibly. Of course, Kyle had grown up fishing on the river. He'd know what was possible or not.

"Plus," Maynard continued, "he's back and forth to Vancouver all the time. I think he's got a girlfriend. Doesn't want to tell people in case they get suspicious why he's moved on so fast."

"Well, I don't have much to do with Jake. He's just a customer."

"Good. Keep it that way."

How likely was it that the police, who had cleared Jake of all suspicion, had gotten it wrong? On the day of the hike, she'd been exactly like Maynard—jumping to conclusions without hearing all the facts. She'd cut Jake off mid-sentence and literally run away. As for taking trips to Vancouver—if she'd had to live with this kind of gossip, she'd want to escape now and then as well.

She hung up her uniform. "See you tomorrow."

Maynard nodded and Kyle gave a wave. She needed to stop thinking about Jake and focus on her own life. Maybe even have a little fun. She got into her car and drove to the motel.

Chapter 7

IT HAD BEEN AGES SINCE MAGGIE HAD BEEN OUT WITH A friend near her own age. Lily arrived, wearing a red T-shirt and a black miniskirt. With her high cheekbones, dark brown eyes, and black hair pulled into a bun, she looked like a model.

"Hey, girlfriend," she said.

"You look great," Maggie said.

"Thanks. So do you."

They walked across the courtyard, dodging playing children, and got into Lily's older-model Honda Civic.

"No one gets to the bar before nine," Lily said. "Let's take a drive to the lookout."

"There's a lookout that you can drive to?" This was news.

Lily turned the key. "Which lookout are you talking about?"

"Jake and I went to one. North of here." She wasn't going to say what a terrible day it had been.

"Ah. No, this is another lookout. You can drive right up. He took you to the best one, though."

They drove out to the highway and exited onto Brantford Road, one the few roads that Maggie had not yet explored. They wound their way up through meadows sprouting daisies, dandelions, and sagebrush. Lily chatted about her dream of moving to Kamloops to go to school, and Maggie described her experiences as a busy restaurant chef.

As the sun started to sink behind the hills, Lily pointed across a meadow. "Look!"

An enormous buck stood at the back of the meadow near the forest, its head held high and alert, its horns majestic.

Lily pulled the car over on the gravel shoulder. "Get a picture."

Maggie pulled out her phone and reached for the door handle.

"Don't close the door," Lily said. "It might spook the deer."

Maggie tiptoed out then held up her phone and snapped the picture. Even with the zoom it was a little too far away, so she crept forward slowly. Turning around, she saw that Lily had gotten out as well. "Is it dangerous?" Maggie whispered.

Lily kept her eyes on the buck. She shook her head slightly.

Maggie snapped another picture. Miraculously, the animal didn't move. Another picture. Closer and closer. She wondered when it would turn and bolt, but it seemed frozen as it stared across the field. Could there be a doe in the vicinity? Maggie was still taking little leaps toward it, crouching for photo after photo, when Lily started to laugh.

Maggie stood up and turned around. Lily was now doubled over with laughter. Maggie looked back to the buck. It still didn't move.

Lily ran up behind her. "It's a decoy."

"A what?"

"A decoy. It's used to catch hunters who give in to the temptation to take a shot from their trucks or hunt out of season. I'm sorry, but Maggie, you are such a city slicker—I just had to take advantage of you. It's a little practical joke we play on newcomers around here."

Maggie glanced down at her phone with all the pictures of the majestic animal. It clearly had not moved at all. Her chuckle grew to a belly laugh when she realized how ridiculous she must have looked.

"Come on. I'll show you," Lily said.

The buck was riddled with bullet holes.

"This was a real buck, though?" Maggie asked.

"Of course. Taxidermy. It's even got bulletproof material under its stuffing."

"This really works?"

"Look at the bullet holes. Each one represents a fine. The game wardens won't be out tonight, but they'll be here tomorrow." Lily smiled. "Come on. I'll show you the blind they use."

To one side of the buck, disguised by foliage, was a cement blind where the wardens could watch the road and wait for an unsuspecting hunter to give in to temptation.

"If the hunters have a gun, isn't that a little dangerous for the wardens?" Maggie asked.

Lily placed her hands on her hips and cocked her head. "Wildlife protection officers are authorized to carry rifles and handguns."

Maggie walked around the buck and touched its side. She felt sad that this noble animal had once been alive, but hunting was a way of life in these parts, and at least the game wardens were giving the animals a fighting chance against some yahoos in a truck.

"Now that you've been initiated into Rosetown," Lily said, "I'm going to buy you a beer."

"What about the lookout?"

Lily smiled. "There isn't one."

Jake sat in the dimly lit bar with Glenn, Mike, and Eric. He rarely came out for this type of thing, but he owed these guys big time. They were going to take over his business while he went to Vancouver to look after Cassie. He'd recruited Mike and Eric from another well-known rafting company and had to offer a pretty good wage to entice them, but at least his passengers would be kept safe while he was away. Jake raised his hand. When the waitress came over, he ordered another round of beers. He, as the designated driver, ordered another 7Up.

He leaned back in his chair and listened to the band play. They were pretty good. They all had other jobs here in town but liked to have a gig on a Saturday night. Tamara Swift, the singer, had shown up at his door with a casserole after Jasmine disappeared. She'd asked him out, but he'd declined. She was a good-looking woman, but her pushiness grated on his nerves.

And then Lily Thomas and Maggie Jackson walked through the door, and Jake could almost feel the testosterone level at his table rise. Maggie's hair was a mass of curls around her face. She was a knockout with her big hazel-green eyes and that blouse tucked into a pair of tight jeans, and there was Lily in a red T-shirt and mini-skirt, tall and slim with almond-shaped eyes. The two were laughing like old friends as they made their way to the bar. A pang hit Jake in his core. Jasmine had never made one friend in this town. She'd never even tried.

The music stopped, and the vocalist announced that they were going to take a short break. Maggie turned around on the bar stool. When she saw him, her face went serious for a minute, but then she gave him a wide smile. He smiled and nodded back.

The bar was decorated with items from the pioneer days. Butter churns, coffee grinders, and colorful glass bottles that had once held tonics were displayed on shelves. Wagon wheels and black-and-white photographs adorned the walls. The bar itself was on the lower floor of the historic Rosetown Hotel. This was a far cry from the clubs Maggie had frequented in Vancouver. But hey—according to Lily, she'd been initiated and was now a full-fledged member of this town.

Behind her sat Jake Jones with a bunch of gorgeous-looking men who were built just like him.

Lily took a sip of beer and leaned in. "I went out with Glenn, the one on the right."

"The rafting pilot?"

"Yeah. He's here from New Zealand on a one-year work visa."

The female vocalist from the band walked over to Jake and placed both hands on his shoulders. She was a good-looking platinum blonde with hoop earrings and a low-cut little black dress. She leaned down to say something to him, in the process exposing her cleavage to all the men at the table, who were doing everything but letting their tongues hang out. Maggie must have frowned, because Lily looked over. The woman was laughing now, her head close to Jake, who was fiddling with his glass, turning it round and round and round.

"Jealous?" Lily asked.

Maggie straightened her back. "Of course not."

"That's Tamara Swift. She's a single mom. Works at the insurance office part-time and does gigs on the weekend." Lily looked Maggie up and down. "She doesn't hold a candle to you."

"Thanks."

When the band started up again, Glenn strolled over and asked Lily to dance. As they walked away, Maggie turned to her half-empty beer, uncomfortable with Jake sitting over there. She was *definitely* jealous, and Tamara Swift's wonderful singing voice made it even worse. Maggie couldn't even carry a tune. She was just about to tell Lily she was heading home when Jake slid onto the bar stool beside her.

"Come here often?" he asked.

Maggie smiled at the trite pickup line. "Not really. You?"

"Nope. But I'm glad I came tonight."

"Why?"

He smiled. "Because you're here."

Maggie turned her knees around to face him. "Maynard thinks you killed your wife."

He sighed and met her eyes. "So do a lot of people. But I never laid a hand on her. And since we're being frank, I think you're here for a reason as well. Who comes to a town like this without knowing a soul, gets a job immediately, says they're staying for exactly four months, and calls it an extended holiday?" He raised his brows and waited.

"You're right. I'm hiding out." There, she'd said it. She'd finally told someone.

"Who from?"

"An ex-boyfriend who happens to be in trouble with the law."

Lily came back. "Don't let me interrupt you," she said.

Jake and Maggie exchanged a look. This wasn't the place to share information.

A slow song started. Jake reached for Maggie's hand and led her onto the dance floor, and as they shared their confessions, they found their way into each other's arms.

"Did this boyfriend hurt you?" Jake whispered in her ear.

"He almost destroyed me." She leaned her head against his chest, and he enveloped her in his arms. "I'll tell you more, but not tonight. Tonight I just need to forget about him."

They swayed to the music. It felt incredibly good to feel his hand move to her waist. At the end of the song, she met his eyes. He didn't say a word, just leaned down and kissed her lightly on the lips. A warmth washed over her, and she wanted to kiss him again but this was neither the time nor the place. He took her hand as they walked back to his table, where Lily had joined the river rafting staff. By the end of the evening, Jake had invited Maggie on a rafting trip the following Tuesday, Glenn had offered his undying love to Lily, and Maggie was quite sure there was a sit-down, tell-all conversation with Jake in her near future.

Chapter 8

WHEN MAGGIE ARRIVED AT THE LAUNCHING DOCK, WEARING her turquoise bikini under a tank top and shorts, Jake was already there talking to Glenn. He looked over. "Hey! What a day."

"It's beautiful," she answered. There wasn't a cloud in the sky. An osprey circled overhead, and the river looked flat and green with twirls of current playing on the surface. Mark and two teenage boys, Thomas and George, drove up in a truck. Next a car pulled up. Maggie recognized Connie's friend, Charlene, but the woman with her was unfamiliar. The two stepped out and walked over to Maggie. Charlene had short gray hair and a big smile. The woman with her had a slim, shapely figure, black curly hair pulled back into a ponytail, and sparkling brown eyes. She looked to be in her mid-forties. Come to think of it, Maggie had seen her around town.

"This is Gabriela. Gabriela, Maggie," Charlene said.

Gabriela extended her hand. "Pleased to meet you." She had a strong Spanish accent.

"Nice to meet you, too. Where are you from? I mean originally."

"Mexico. Have you ever been there?"

Maggie smiled. "Just once, to Puerto Vallarta."

"I'm from Guadalajara."

Glenn handed each of them a life jacket and paddle. He explained that they would sit on the rounded, inflated sides of the raft with one foot in the boat and the other foot resting just above the water. "See the rope that runs around the perimeter of the raft? That's what you grab onto if you feel yourself slipping. You'll hear me yell, 'paddle left,' 'paddle right,' or 'paddle all.' When I tell you to paddle, you paddle like your life depends on it."

Mark paled.

Jake walked over. "And when Glenn gives the order to get down, get yourselves and your paddles into the center of the boat. These orders are non-negotiable. Your safety depends on following them." He was talking to the group, but his eyes lingered on the two distracted teenage boys who clearly wanted to be out on the rapids as quickly as possible.

"When I say 'clear,' you can come back up and paddle again," Glenn said. "Now here's what's really important: if you do fall overboard—especially into white water—and you feel an undertow pulling you down, don't fight it. Hold your breath, because in a minute or two, you'll bob back up. It's just the way the river works. Jake will be following in the chase boat, and he'll pick you up. Any questions?"

"Is there a place I can store my glasses?" Mark asked.

"Sure. Give me your wallets, glasses, or anything else that you don't want to risk losing, and I'll store them in the waterproof container under my seat."

Only Mark handed over his glasses. Everyone else seemed to have left their personal belongings locked in their cars.

"All right, then," Glenn said. "Let's get on board."

Maggie, Charlene, and Thomas sat on one side of the raft while Gabriela, Mark, and George sat on the other side. Glenn sat at the back, holding the two long pilot paddles. Jake gave them a push out into the river, where they practiced paddling in a circle first to the left and then to the right. They practiced easing themselves down into the center of the boat. Then they were asked to paddle in a figure eight. Jake started the engine on the chase boat and steered it out behind them.

They paddled quietly for the first twenty minutes, just absorbing the sun and observing the rusty-brown cliffs.

"Hey," Jake called out. He pointed to the far bank of the river.

A black bear and her two cubs were making their way toward the water. As the raft drew nearer, the mother bear looked up, decided her audience was of no consequence to her, and continued her lopsided journey down the steep bank. One of the cubs rolled down the sandy slope, and the other cub tumbled down behind it. It felt almost magical, this combination of sky, water, birds, and bears.

The river began to pick up speed, and a large jutting rock appeared. "Paddle left!" Glenn shouted. Maggie, Charlene, and Thomas all paddled furiously. They had just cleared the rock when Glenn shouted, "Paddle all, paddle all!"

They were bouncing up and down in the frothing river. Maggie alternated between paddling and clinging to the rope like she was holding the reins of a bucking bronco. With each wave, she bounced into the air and landed on the soft and slippery side of the boat. Charlene was laughing and enjoying herself. Mark looked terrified. Gabriela lay face down on the rubber edge, bouncing like a fish on a line and muttering either prayers or expletives in Spanish. Thomas and George whooped as each wave hit. In fact, they were probably the strongest paddlers of the whole crew. Glenn and Jake occasionally exchanged hand signals, only a few of which Maggie could understand.

The boat took a twist. "Get down, get down!" Glenn yelled.

Mark lost his balance and landed on his back in the center of the raft. Gabriela bounced and landed on top of him. Everyone else managed to crouch in the middle, still holding the side rope as the waves splashed over them. Gabriela rolled off Mark, and he used his one arm, still pinned under her, to pull her into a sitting position. The boat took a skyward bounce.

"Mother of God," Gabriela said.

"Jesus," Mark added. He glanced at the two teenagers. "I'm not swearing. I'm just asking for help."

"Clear," Glenn yelled. "Good work, mates. Now back up to your stations."

Maggie loved every minute of frantic paddling, riding the bronco, and throwing herself into the center of the boat. Two hours passed. The river calmed, and they floated with the current. Up ahead, she saw a rocky beach with a trail up the embankment to a level area, where a teenage boy was waving to them. A house stood on the bluff, but the lower floor was built right into the slope, like it was part of the hill itself. They paddled their raft out of the downward current, pulled up to a wooden dock, and hopped out. Glenn reached into the box under the seat and handed Mark his glasses.

Mark put them on and smiled. "Well, that was more fun than church on Sunday!"

"Way more fun," Maggie teased.

"For me, that was just like church," Gabriela said.

"My goodness," Mark said. "Father Norman must have some pretty exciting things happening over at your church."

"Not exactly. He just likes to remind us that we're going to die. It was foremost in my mind today as well."

Mark chuckled.

Jake pulled up to the dock and jumped from his boat. Susie bounded down the hill. He rubbed her ears. "Hey, girl."

This was Jake's house. It suited him.

"You did great," Jake said to the group. "The rest of the trip is smooth as glass compared to that first bit, so relax and enjoy your lunch. Sammy has everything ready for us." They walked up the trail to a gravel parking lot, where a few picnic tables were laid out with buns, cold cuts, cheese, lettuce, tomatoes, and some cookies. Sammy, who was filling glasses with lemonade, motioned that they should help themselves.

Maggie took a sip of the cool liquid. "You work for Jake?" she asked.

Sammy smiled. "Jake's hired me for the summer. I love it. I get to meet people from all around the world. Girls too." Sammy had on a clean white T-shirt and a pair of jeans. With his spiked black hair and doe-brown eyes, the teenage girls probably enjoyed meeting him as well.

"Sounds like fun."

Maggie made a sandwich, and Gabriela and Mark joined her.

"I'll suggest river rafting to my daughter," Gabriela said. "She loves adventure."

"How old is she?" Maggie asked.

"Carmela is sixteen. My son, Alfonso, is eighteen. They live with me, but go visit their father. I'm divorced, you see."

"Does your ex live in town?"

"Yes, have you met him? He has blond hair and blue eyes—he's a bodybuilder." Gabriela reached for a handful of grapes.

A man who fit the description had been trying to flirt with Maggie at the restaurant—despite the wedding ring on his finger. Maggie placed her sandwich on a plate. "Yes, I think I may have met him. Did he remarry?"

Gabriela popped a grape in her mouth. "Yes. Poor woman."

Mark had his glasses off and was vigorously rubbing them with a tissue.

Gabriela turned to him. "We are quite a prayer team, no?"

He put on his glasses. "We did seem to be the only two people on the boat calling for divine intervention. I think we had it covered."

Gabriela laughed, a light, happy sound. "Aren't you eating?"

"I was just giving my stomach a few minutes to settle." He reached for a bun and added a slice of turkey and a piece of cheese.

Gabriela studied Mark as he slathered mayonnaise onto the bun. "Perhaps you'd like to come over and see my art studio?"

His Adam's apple bobbed. When he turned to face her, he looked like a hopeful child. "Yes, I could bring some lunch or dinner."

Gabriela tipped her head. "No, I'll cook something. Do you like things hot and spicy?"

Mark turned pink. "Sure, I like spice."

"Good. I'll make Mexican food."

Realizing that she was no longer part of this conversation, Maggie left them alone to work out the details. She walked over to Charlene, who was talking to George and Thomas. The three of them were totally pumped about the second half of the trip.

Jake joined them, munching on an apple. "When you're finished, feel free to go up to the house and use the facilities, and then we'll get back out on the boats."

Maggie helped Sammy carry the trays of dishes to the house. A white MG convertible was parked in the carport. *Jasmine's car.* Jake probably couldn't sell it if it was registered in his wife's name. Maggie shook her head. What a situation to be in.

She followed Sammy into a modern kitchen and placed the dishes on the counter.

Sammy pointed to a hallway. "The bathroom is down there on the right."

On her way back out, with Sammy nowhere in sight, she stopped in the living room to admire the view of the river and rolling hills. She turned to leave, and a silver-framed photograph caught her eye. The little girl had curly black hair, a big smile, and looked to be no more than four or five years of age. Was she a relative? She must be someone special, since it was the only photo in the whole room. Maggie glanced out the window to see people donning their life jackets. She hurried outside, closing the door behind her.

Ten minutes later, they were back on the raft, bobbing up and down in the river.

As the river widened and the rapids decreased, Jake pulled his boat up beside them. "Feel free to jump out and swim if you like. This part of the river is safe."

George and Thomas whooped and dived overboard. Charlene eased herself over the edge and floated, keeping a tight grip on the rope. Mark and Gabriela stayed on board. Maggie deliberately fell sideways into the water and bobbed up a few feet away. She swam over to Jake.

"How's the water?" he asked.

"Refreshing. Are you coming in?"

"Not when I'm on duty." He looked at her for a minute, as if deciding something. "Come to my place for supper tomorrow night."

She clutched the side of his boat. His blue eyes were serious, and for a brief second, she wished he'd pull her into the boat and she could apologize for being such a jerk. "What can I bring?"

He smiled. "Not a thing. Six o'clock OK?"

"OK." She pushed off and swam away.

Chapter

9

JAKE AND MAGGIE SAT OUTSIDE ON THE DECK DESPITE THE weather. A mixture of dark and gray clouds had moved in, but the air was still warm from the day.

Jake took a sip of beer. "So you enjoyed the trip yesterday?"

"It was great." She frowned a little. "I'm not sure that Mark and Gabriela enjoyed it."

He cocked his head. "Fear brings people together."

"You were matchmaking?" She looked incredulous.

"Of course."

"I think it worked. Gabriela asked him if he liked things hot and spicy." She lifted her brows.

Jake laughed and got up to put the steaks on the barbecue. Susie, who'd been sitting by Maggie, shifted her position to give Jake a woeful look.

Maggie smiled. "I think she wants a steak." Susie's tail thumped against the deck.

"Probably, but she's getting kibble. Come on, Susie."

He stepped into the laundry room off the kitchen and fed the dog. He wasn't going to attempt any deep conversation until after they'd eaten. His story would ruin anyone's digestion. He grabbed the bottle of red wine from the counter before stepping back outside.

Maggie was leaning on the deck railing, looking out at the river. Her hair blew in the breeze, her waist looked small, and her hips . . . He caught himself before he could take those thoughts further. Wouldn't it be nice if just once he could be a normal guy inviting a woman over for supper and whatever else that might lead to?

She turned and caught his gaze. "Can I help with anything?"

"No, you relax. How do you like your steak?"

"Medium rare."

"Me too." He picked up the tongs and flipped the meat over.

A few minutes later, he was serving up the garlic bread and Caesar salad. He handed her a plate, which she balanced on her knees, her glass of red wine sitting on the white plastic end table. She sliced off a piece of steak, put it in her mouth, and closed her eyes. "Delicious."

"Glad you like it. It's hard to impress a chef."

"I'm impressed. You even made your own dressing."

He glanced at the untouched salad on her plate. "You can tell just by looking at it?"

"I can tell some things, but not everything." She nibbled a romaine leaf. "Yes, the perfect amount of anchovy. You got this right."

"Thanks." He was pleased. He'd made three attempts at that dressing. He bit into the steak. It felt good sitting here with the river running by, the hills before them dotted with pine and sage. Too bad they both had skeletons in the closet. Too bad they had to open those closet doors.

She took a sip of wine. "Thomas and George loved the rafting."

Jake didn't mention that the boys had taken the trip for free, thanks to Mark's persuasion. Mark had convinced him that giving the boys a rafting experience, which neither they nor their families could afford, would be tantamount to a charitable donation to the church. In the end, Jake was glad he'd agreed. Both boys had been strong paddlers, and even more importantly, they'd shown respect for the river. They were only fifteen years old, but in a few years' time they'd be potential employees. "How was work today?"

"Fine. I'll be in charge for the next three days." She gave him a mischievous look.

"You like to be in charge?"

"I do."

"Me too."

Jake met her eyes, an unspoken question playing in his mind. How would they be as a couple? A dynamite duo or two bulls locking horns? A little of each was his wager. "Would you like to own your own restaurant someday?"

"That's my dream." She sliced off another piece of steak. "What about you? Which job do you like best? Electrician or business owner?"

"The rafting business wins hands down, although I probably earn more as an electrician. What I'd like to do is find a way to get the tourists up here in the fall and winter. The wildlife viewing and photography are better then. If you want to see a moose, come in October."

She tilted her head. "Why?"

Jake thought of the previous autumn—being out in the bush alone. He'd heard the moose, followed the sound, climbed a tree and pulled out his binoculars. He'd watched the males charging at one another, tangling their horns to decide who would mate. "It's rutting season. Plus, the snowy owls come down from the Arctic in the winter. I could take tourists out on snowshoes to see them."

"Wouldn't you need night-vision goggles?"

Jake laughed at the image. "Nope. They're one of the few owls that are not nocturnal."

She slowly nodded her head. "I think with a little advertising, you could do very well."

"I just haven't had the time to put the effort into it. But someday . . . hopefully." He picked up her empty plate. "I'll be right back."

He served up two pieces of strawberry-rhubarb pie with vanilla ice-cream. When he stepped back out, she had her phone out.

"Speaking of wildlife, take a look at this."

He scrolled through the photos and started to laugh. "The decoy."

"Lily took me there."

He gave her a sideways glance. "Looks like you got pretty close to the beast."

She laughed. "Totally."

He put a hand on her shoulder. "That means you're initiated into this town."

She looked up. "Did you fall for it?"

"No. I'm from Beaver Lake. We know about decoys. Glenn fell for it, though. I'll bet she took you out there at dusk, when it was just a little hard to see."

"She did. It was the same night that we showed up at the bar."

"No wonder Lily was in such good spirits. She'd just had another victim." A drop of rain hit his arm. "Let's move inside."

They ate their pie at the kitchen island then Maggie rinsed the plates, and he loaded them into the dishwasher. It felt so right to be standing beside her, doing this menial task. It would be nice to forget all about talking, build a fire, and explore her body with his hands. It *would* be nice—but it wouldn't be right. She needed to know what she'd be getting herself into. "Coffee?" he asked.

"Sure." She tucked her hair nervously behind one ear. At the bar, it had taken all his restraint to only kiss her once. With all the emotion pent up inside him, he wanted to kiss her again, but instead, he scooped some coffee into the coffee maker and set it to brew. She wiped down the counter like she was trying to avoid the share-all as much as he was. But a few minutes later, he handed her a cup of coffee, and they made their way to the living room. Rain pounded on the roof. Jake stacked some wood in the fireplace and lit it.

When he sat beside her, she touched his hand. "Shall I go first?"

He'd wanted to get his stuff over with so that when she rejected him, he could start the recovery process right away. On other hand, the mention of a criminal boyfriend had spiked his curiosity. "Go ahead."

She began by telling him her number one mistake: dating the boss. Then she told him about her number two mistake: falling in love with the boss. "What I didn't know was that Carlo was using his connections in Colombia to smuggle drugs through the port of Vancouver. I often picked up supplies for him. I wasn't hired for this—I was hired as a chef—but when you date the boss . . . well, all the boundaries become blurred."

Jake nodded, like he got the concept.

"One day, I was driving home from the port when I was pulled over by the Vancouver Police. There was a five-kilogram bag of cocaine hidden in the box of coffee beans on the front seat." She paused to gauge his reaction.

"Whoa." Jake shook his head. "He set you up."

"Yes." It all seemed so clear, but she couldn't blame Carlo entirely. She might as well tell him the whole truth. "Jake, even before I was arrested, I had begun to suspect he was drug dealing, and I carried on anyway. He was always on the phone to Colombia. There were way too many supplies coming in that could have been locally sourced. I even caught him loading wads of cash into the restaurant safe. He said it was money he'd won at the casino."

Jake tipped his head and lifted his brows.

"I know. Stupid. I didn't believe him, but I wanted it to be true. After that, I started to snap pictures of his friends and keep track of all the deliveries that came to the restaurant." She thought back to the stress of those days and gave an involuntary shudder.

"Why?"

"Deep down, I knew I was going to be implicated. I needed bargaining tools." In other words, she'd been a hair's breadth away from knowing the truth. A smarter person would have figured it out. Or maybe *wiser* was the better word.

"So what happened after you were pulled over?"

"I was taken to jail, where I spent my twenty-fifth birthday. After a week's stay, I made a deal with the police: I'd hand over all my information and testify against Carlo, and they'd drop all charges against me. They arrested Carlo. The court date is set for September seventeenth. If I don't show, I'll be charged with possession of drugs with intent to traffic."

"So if Carlo is locked up, why are you here?"

"He made bail."

Jake whistled. "I get it."

Outside, the sky was darkening, and the river disappeared into a dark shadow. "I was offered police protection, but I didn't trust the police. Carlo had too much influence. Possibly even a few crooked cops on the payroll. The officer in charge of my case knows I'm here, but it's a locked file. Other police officers can't access it. He informed my family that I'm in hiding. I don't make any phone calls outside of this town or go on the Internet. I'm off the grid, so to speak."

Jake put a warm hand over hers. "I'm curious. Why didn't you leave Carlo when you suspected he wasn't on the up and up?"

He'd just asked the question she'd asked herself a million times. "I thought about it, but I didn't do it." A lump rose to her throat. She'd been such an idiot.

Jake squeezed her hand. "It's all right. I was just curious. The one thing I still don't get is, why Rosetown?"

"Carlo has conditions attached to his bail. One, he's forbidden from leaving Vancouver, and two, he has to check in with pre-trial services every twenty-four hours, or he forfeits the bail bond. I didn't have a car in Vancouver. I always borrowed Carlo's, so the day he made bail, I bought the Plymouth station wagon and drove out of town. I guess I was in a panic, because I just kept driving. When I pulled into the Ponderosa Motel, something told me I'd had enough, and this town would be as good as the next."

Jake lifted her hand to his lips. "I'm glad you're here."

"Even though I'm a dumbass idiot?"

Jake chuckled. "Would you like some more coffee?"

She felt tense. "Maybe a glass of wine instead."

"Sure. I'll have one, too." He walked to the kitchen and came back with a bottle of red wine and two glasses. He poured them each a glass and set the bottle aside. "Now I'll tell you a story that'll prove you're not the only dumbass idiot in this town."

Chapter 10

(handwritten margin note: Jack > Cassie / Jasmin)

JAKE HANDED MAGGIE THE FRAMED PHOTO OF CASSIE. "THIS is my stepdaughter. She lives in Vancouver with Jasmine's mother."

Maggie examined the picture. "I never heard that you had a child."

"Jasmine didn't want anyone to know. Cassie never lived with us, and Jasmine was embarrassed about that."

Maggie placed the picture on the coffee table. "How old is Cassie?"

"She just turned six."

"And you keep in touch?"

"Yes. That's why I'm back and forth to Vancouver all the time. Mark knows about her, and so do the RCMP officers in charge of the investigation. But no one else. I'm the target of enough gossip. Why fuel it more?"

Jake ran a hand through his hair. Where to begin? Probably with his marriage proposal—the day he'd been the biggest dumbass idiot of all. Telling Maggie this was like wading into water and not stopping until it was way over his head, but it had to be done. "I met Jasmine in Kamloops three and a half years ago.

I was working as an electrician at the plywood mill, and she was taking college courses to become a legal assistant. We had a whirlwind romance, and I asked her to marry me after only six months."

"Wow," Maggie said.

"I know it was impulsive, but I was crazy about her. Probably because she was everything I was not. She seemed sophisticated. I saw myself as a country bumpkin. She introduced me to fine dining, live theater, and classical music." Maggie cocked her head, a little disbelief in her eyes, and he chuckled. "Not that I took to the classical music part."

"I didn't think so."

"Two months after the engagement, we were married in a Las Vegas chapel." Her eyes grew round. "I know—crazy. I was wasted, but still sober enough to protest when she asked me to marry her on the spur of the moment. She convinced me by saying the ceremony would be quiet and simple, just the way she'd dreamed it would be. In my drunken state, I figured we were going to get married anyway, and if this was what she wanted, why not? But I didn't hear about Cassie until we traveled to Vancouver to meet Jasmine's mother, Marie."

"My God. Did Jasmine tell you on the way there?"

"Nope. We arrived at Marie's house, and there Cassie was. Marie had no idea that I hadn't been told. How was I supposed to know that my nineteen-year-old wife had a three-year-old daughter?"

"How old were you?"

"Twenty-five. Old enough to have known better. I should never have gotten married—at least not like that." Jake took a moment to refill their wine glasses. "I was furious at the deception, but Cassie, at three years old, was the cutest kid I'd ever met, and somehow, I got past it."

Maggie's eyes looked understanding, and it gave him courage to go on.

"Anyway, we started to spend our weekends in Vancouver. Cassie and I grew really attached to one another. She started to call me Daddy, and I started to think of her as my daughter. I wanted her to move to Kamloops to be with us, but Jasmine wanted to finish her course first."

"How did Cassie's grandmother feel about that?"

"She was for it. At fifty-three, she was on her own. She and Jasmine's father had been divorced for years, and he no longer had any contact. Marie knew she wasn't up for the long haul of raising a child, but she definitely wanted to stay involved in Cassie's life. In fact, at that time, she was talking about moving to Kamloops."

Maggie put her elbow on the back of the couch and leaned on her hand. "Let me backtrack a little here. Jasmine had Cassie when she was sixteen years old?"

"That's right. She told me that she broke up with her boyfriend when she found out she was pregnant. He went to another school, and she never told him about Cassie. This turned out to be a lie, but I'll get to that later." Jake took a sip of wine and gathered his thoughts. "A year went by, and the mill I worked for closed. Jasmine graduated. We moved to Rosetown, and I started the river rafting business. I wanted to bring Cassie to live with us and legally adopt her, but Jasmine refused."

Maggie knit her brow. "To which? Bringing Cassie to Rosetown or the adoption?"

"Both. Marie was ready to sell up in Vancouver and buy a house here. She was going to do all the babysitting. It was a win-win situation, but Jasmine phoned Marie and told her not to come. *Period.*"

Jake paused. The rain had stopped. The fire had burned out, and his back was in knots. "Let's get some fresh air."

He took a couple of jackets and a wool blanket out of the closet. Susie, sensing movement, left her dog bed and joined them. Jake helped Maggie into an oversized coat then extended his hand, and they walked down to the beach.

Chapter 11

BLACK SMOKY CLOUDS DRIFTED ACROSS A FULL MOON. Maggie looked up at the clear patches where the stars twinkled. Susie came back from the water's edge and lay down between them on the blanket. Jake ruffled the dog's fur. "Cassie and I bought Susie in Vancouver. Cassie picked the name."

Now she understood why a guy like him had a dog named Susie. She picked up a pebble and threw it into the moonlit water. "I don't get it. Why wouldn't Jasmine want Cassie to come live with you?"

"I didn't get it either. We still traveled back and forth to Vancouver all the time, but now, I was the one to take Cassie to the playground or the beach, while Jasmine was out doing who knows what. She'd come home after Cassie was in bed." Jake's lips formed a tight line. "She was a terrible mother."

"Did she ever hit Cassie?"

"Never, but the neglect was emotional abuse. Cassie turned five, and I was sick and tired of the long drive back and forth when we could all live in one location. My marriage was on the rocks, but if

I took a stand and left, Jasmine would have made sure that I never saw Cassie again."

"Why?"

"Because she was crazy and spiteful. She had no problem using her own daughter to manipulate me."

Maggie let it all sink in. "Couldn't Marie have given you access to Cassie? I mean, if you separated or divorced?"

He shook his head. "Marie walked on eggshells around her daughter. I talked to her about it one day, and she told me that Jasmine couldn't help her behavior. She said Jasmine couldn't attach to Cassie because of something bad that had happened. I asked if Jasmine had been raped. If Cassie were the result, that would explain Jasmine's rejection of her."

"Was it was true?"

Jake shook his head. "No. Cassie was the result of a promiscuous fifteen-year-old who'd been with so many boys that even she didn't know who the father was." He paused. "But that's not all Marie told me. Jasmine had been sexually abused by her father. She was only twelve years old when Marie found out."

"That's horrible. No wonder Jasmine was so messed up."

"It explained a lot. Marie threatened to press charges unless her husband left and never contacted them again. They've never heard from him since."

"But Marie should have pressed charges."

"Damn right, she should have. Her excuse was that Tom was a good salesman, and if he could sell his own innocence, he'd still have access to Jasmine. She couldn't risk it. The weird thing is that after Marie told me this, I asked Jasmine about her father, and she said he'd been a pretty good dad before the marriage broke up."

"What did you say?"

"Nothing. Marie made me promise to not tell Jasmine what I knew. She said that every time she tried to bring up the past to Jasmine, Jasmine would shut her out entirely—for weeks, sometimes even months. She didn't want me driving any more wedges between them."

Maggie threw another pebble into the river. "That's a heck of a secret to keep in a marriage."

"Believe me, it took its toll. I now understood a little more about why Jasmine was the way she was, but it didn't make living together any easier." Jake put his hand on the sleeping dog between them. "Because of Cassie, I decided to make one last-ditch effort to save my marriage." He glanced over. "Are you cold?"

She shivered. "I am."

Jake rose and extended his hand, pulling her to her feet. "Let's go back to the house."

They walked up the path, each lost in their own thoughts.

Inside, they sat at the kitchen island. "Water?" he asked.

"Sure." He handed her a glass and she took a sip. "Go on."

He gave her an embarrassed smile. "First, I spent a month acting like I was in love—bringing Jasmine flowers, taking her out, and refusing to fight about anything. After the buttering up was done, I started talking about Cassie and Marie moving here in a really positive way. No confrontation—just how nice it would be to have Easter egg hunts and be in our own house Christmas morning with a huge tree we'd chopped down ourselves.

"Finally, I took her out to lunch, just to avoid a big scene if things went south. I told her that I wanted to bring Cassie home. I thought, maybe this time, the answer would be different." He paused.

"So what happened?"

"She told me to go to hell." Jake gave her a rueful smile. "For someone who didn't want a public scene, I sure made one. All the disappointment and frustration just took over. I slammed my fist on the table. I told her that I was done. I walked out and left her sitting there. She chased me out to my truck a few minutes later and begged me to take her home. We arrived at the house, and I headed straight for the river. I was going out on the boat. I didn't want to be near her, but she ran after me, saying she wanted to talk."

Jake picked up his glass of water and downed it before continuing.

"She told me that she'd resented Cassie ever since she'd had her. She felt the baby had robbed her of her freedom, and she'd been fighting to get it back ever since. She understood that it wasn't Cassie's fault, and she wanted to get past it. She suggested that we bring Cassie home and just muddle our way through it—like a family."

Maggie bit her lip and waited for him to go on.

"We took a trip down the river, and when we got home, I went to bed and fell soundly asleep for the first time in months. When I woke up, Jasmine wasn't there. She wasn't in the house, so I went outside. Her car was there. I figured she'd gone for a walk, but I was worried. Jasmine wasn't a morning person, and she wasn't much of a walker, either. I called and texted her all day from work, with no reply. That afternoon, I called Marie, but she hadn't heard anything. That night, I filed a missing person's report." He got up and walked over to the window, looking out for a moment before turning. "An investigation followed. People had overheard our argument at Maynard's, so I was questioned, but they cleared me when the dogs tracked her to the highway—where the scent suddenly stopped. She had gotten into a car. Maybe hitchhiked with someone who was bad news."

"Why hitchhike? She had a car."

"Good question. You had to know her."

"What do you mean?"

He looked like he was searching for the right words. "One time, we were rafting, just the two of us, and she jumped into the rapids. I pulled her out, but I was furious. There was no pilot boat, and if I hadn't moved quickly, I wouldn't have been able to save her. She had this blank look in her eyes. It was almost like she wanted to die."

The story was becoming more bizarre by the minute. "So she was impulsive?"

Jake shrugged. "Yeah. More like insane."

Maggie thought of what Connie had told her during their lunch. "Did Jasmine have any friends?"

He shook his head. "Not that I knew of."

"So what does Cassie know about all this?"

"She knows that her mother is missing, and the police are looking for her. Fortunately, she doesn't ask too many questions, since Jasmine never spent much time with her anyway. Cassie is attached to Marie, and she's attached to me. She was never really attached to her mother."

Maggie tilted her head. "So is this how it ends? With you being a long-distance father for the rest of your life?"

Jake met her eyes. "It's a little more complicated than that. Marie has ovarian cancer. We were already making plans for her and Cassie to move to Rosetown when the diagnosis came in. She's scheduled for surgery then chemotherapy. She has to stay in Vancouver, at least for the time being. I'm leaving tomorrow to take care of Cassie while she has the surgery and recovers."

This was news. "How long will you be gone?"

"At least three weeks." He paused, and his face became so serious that her heart began to pound.

"There's more, isn't there?"

"Yes. If Marie dies, Cassie will be handed over to her next-closest living relative—her grandfather, Tom Schmidt.

Maggie gasped. "Jasmine's father?"

"Yes."

"Surely no one would turn her over to an abuser."

"Remember, no charges were laid at the time. Marie and I have talked about trying to lay them now, but it would be Marie's word against his. And then we'd have to inform him of Cassie's existence, and neither one of us wants to do that."

This was unthinkable. "But you're the stepfather!"

"She's never lived with me, but yes, that will be my argument if it goes to court."

"But can't Marie name you as guardian in her will?"

"Marie doesn't have custody. Jasmine does. The way it stands now, Marie has temporary guardianship until Jasmine shows up."

"But she may never show up."

"Exactly. If she were murdered, there's nothing but bush around here for hundreds of miles. She could never be found. If something happens to Marie, temporary guardianship would pass to Tom Schmidt, Cassie's grandfather."

"But Cassie has never even met him!"

Jake sighed. "If you were a judge, who would you pick? A grandfather who is a blood relative or an unrelated stepfather who has never even lived with the child?"

Maggie shook her head. "I see your point."

He picked up their empty glasses and placed them in the sink. His usually straight shoulders sagged a little. "I'll do whatever it takes to secure Cassie's future. It might cost me all I have, but she's never going to that man."

"You're a good person."

He sat down across from her and smiled. "I'm a dumbass idiot."

Maggie took his hand then glanced at her watch—it was two in the morning. She was going to be exhausted when the alarm rang. "I have to get going. I'm working tomorrow . . . or should I say today?"

"I'll walk you to your car." He picked up one of his jackets. "Want to borrow it?"

She nodded and turned around as he held it out. She was about to step out the door when he pulled her toward him. She took a moment to relax into the hug before stepping back. He gently kissed her lips.

She smiled. "Call me when you get to Vancouver."

He met her eyes. "I will."

Chapter 12

MAGGIE ENTERED THE RESTAURANT AND IMMEDIATELY SET the coffee to brew. She needed caffeine, and she needed it quickly. She hoped that Jake, who was already on the road to Vancouver, felt more alert than she did. She walked to the front window and looked out at the empty street. An idea was forming in the back of her mind.

She opened the deep freeze to see what Maynard had in stock. She dug through the packages of french fries, bacon, and frozen hamburgers. Finally, at the very bottom, she found a large box of New York steaks. Maynard never served steaks. Maybe they were for personal use. Would he mind if she used them? Probably not, as long as she raised the bottom line.

She put the steaks on a tray to defrost. All she needed were some French loaves, and voilà—grilled New York steak served on garlic toast with a side of fries or salad. She was throwing sprigs of parsley into ice water when Kyle walked in, looking exhausted.

"Late night?" she asked.

"Yeah."

"Me too."

Whisper to the River

Kyle turned on the grills. Lily arrived a few minutes later and reached for a uniform from the hook on the wall.

"You don't have to wear that ugly thing," Maggie said. "Maynard is away."

"Oh, right. When the cat's away, the mice will play." Lily left the uniform on the hook and did a little jig as she walked through the doors to the front.

Maggie slipped out to the supermarket and returned with eight loaves of French bread and a bouquet of assorted flowers. She snatched up the vases of plastic flowers that decorated the tables and emptied them. She filled them with water and added a few stems of something fresh. This restaurant needed a face-lift, and she was going to give it one. Besides, the activity kept her from slumping over the counter in weariness.

A few stools over, a retired rancher sat drinking a coffee and waiting for his breakfast. "Say, don't you girls usually wear a uniform?"

"We do."

He peered through the pass-through to the kitchen. "Where's Maynard today?"

She lined the vases up on a tray, ready to go out. "Away."

"Did he OK you dressing like that?"

Maggie glanced down at her clean white T-shirt and jeans, leaned toward him, and lowered her voice. "No, and if you tell him, I'll assume that you like your eggs rubbery and your bacon burnt."

The old rancher chuckled. "He won't be hearing nothing from me."

At lunchtime, customers cautiously smelled the flowers, and Lily told them about the steak special. Some chose to stay with the staid, tried-and-true menu items, but many decided to take a chance on something new. Lily was flirting with a young, good-looking rancher when Glenn walked in.

Maggie grabbed a menu. "Hey, Glenn. How's it going?"

"Good." He glanced at Lily again. He was muscular and tanned with vivid blue eyes and sandy brown hair, but Lily refused to move their relationship beyond casual. She said her plans didn't include a man who was going to hightail it back to New Zealand in eight months' time.

Maggie sat him at a table by the window. "Would you like to try the steak special?"

"Sure," he said in his adorable Kiwi accent. How could Lily resist him?

Ed came in and dropped off Rose. Lily got her daughter seated at the counter and gave her a child's menu to color. "You're not to bother Mommy while she's working. Understand? Grandpa will be back in an hour."

"You can bother me any time you like, though," Maggie said with a smile.

The jingling of bells over the door alerted her to more customers. If it kept up like this, Kyle would need help in the kitchen. A middle-aged man walked in wearing beige dress slacks and a yellow polo shirt. With his goatee and red-framed glasses, he clearly wasn't a local.

Maggie motioned to a table. He took a seat, and she handed him a menu. "We have a steak special today."

He looked up with interest.

"It's served with garlic bread and your choice of fries or salad."

He adjusted his chair. "What are your salads?"

The door opened and another group walked in. "Caesar and house. All the dressings are made right here."

He passed her the menu. "Sold. I'll take it with the Caesar salad, please."

"How do you like your steak?"

"Rare."

Maggie clipped the order on the order wheel. "Do you need help?" she called out to Kyle.

He nodded.

In the kitchen, she braised the newcomer's steak and put it on a plate.

Kyle grimaced. "That looks really rare."

"Trust me. I'm going to let it stand for two minutes. It will continue to cook and lock in the juices." When the two minutes were up, she put the steak on a clean plate then added the garlic bread, Caesar salad, and a sprig of parsley and placed it on the pass-through.

The lunch crowd was starting to die down when she made her way back out to the front. The newcomer beckoned her over. "That was delicious. May I ask what you used to marinate the steak?"

"No, you may not."

He chuckled. "You chefs are all the same."

"Where are you from?"

"Vancouver. I'm a travel writer. I'm working on an article about the interior of British Columbia."

"Have you ever been to Rosetown?"

"Never."

"Make sure you check out the museum and the local swimming hole. We also have some great hikes. The tourist center has maps and brochures."

"I will."

She thought of Jake's idea to promote fall and winter tourism. "And remember, there are all kinds of activities here in the off-season as well—wildlife viewing and snowshoeing. We could be the next Whistler, at a much lower cost."

Lily joined them and filled his water glass.

"Wonderful," he said. "If only you could offer me a glass of cabernet, I'd think I'd died and gone to heaven."

Rose left her coloring on the counter and wandered over. "Mommy, I'm bored."

Lily stroked Rose's braided head. "Grandpa will be back any minute."

The travel writer was studying Lily and Rose, his head tipped to the side. "Excuse me, Miss. Would you mind if I took a picture of you and your daughter to use in an article I'm writing?"

"No, we wouldn't mind."

He pulled a camera out of his satchel. Lily rolled her eyes and made a face that only Maggie would catch. Every outsider who came to town, particularly the Europeans, wanted to take pictures of indigenous people. The younger generation would protest, claiming that tradition said it could bring bad luck. But as soon as they were offered twenty bucks, they'd decide that just one photo wouldn't hurt. Later, they'd hold up their twenty-dollar bill and laugh—as long as one of the elders wasn't around to cuff their heads.

Lily put up a hand. "I've changed my mind. It might be bad for my child."

As if on cue, Rose looked at her mother solemnly. Maggie smiled and walked away.

Ten minutes later the travel writer came up to pay. He pulled out an expensive-looking leather wallet. "Do you own this place?"

"No. I'm the manager." Technically she *was* the manager—for the next three days.

He glanced around. "It's lovely. Small-town ambience with a hint of spice."

She smiled. "Thank you."

Maggie turned the sign to *Closed*. Kyle came out and poured himself a Coke.

"That writer was quite the character," Maggie said to Lily, who was filling the ketchup containers. "How many pictures did he take?"

"Just one." Lily reached into the pocket of her jeans and waved a twenty in the air.

Kyle burst out laughing. Another victim.

Chapter 13

Jake stood at the stove of Marie's small but cozy house and threw a handful of diced carrots into a pot of chicken soup. Marie's surgery had been successful, and she was upstairs resting. So far, not wanting to micromanage, Jake had resisted the urge to call Glenn and check on the rafting business. In the week he'd been here, he'd only called Maggie three times because he didn't want to turn her off by looking too eager. On the other hand, he didn't want to look uninterested. Finding that perfect balance was never easy.

He walked into the living room. Stuffed animals lay everywhere, but Cassie was nowhere in sight. He heard a bark from Susie then the squeak of bedsprings. He took the stairs two at a time and found Cassie jumping up and down on the end of Marie's bed. He reached out and caught her. She giggled.

Marie looked pale. "She came to keep me company, that's all."

"Cassie, you can't jump on the bed. Grandma has to recover."

"I was asleep when she came in." Marie smiled at Cassie. "I guess you got bored waiting for me to wake up. Right?"

Cassie nodded.

Marie opened her arms. "Come here."

Jake put Cassie down, and she ran into her grandmother's arms. "Sorry," he said. "I was making chicken soup."

Marie smiled. "Don't worry about it."

Jake extended his hand to Cassie. "Come on. Let's let Grandma get some rest." He closed the bedroom door behind them.

Later that evening, Jake took Cassie to the beach for a swim—his plan to tire her out. When they came out of the water, he picked her up, threw her over his shoulder and jogged down the beach with her bouncing and giggling all the way.

After he put her down, she grabbed his hand. "More, Daddy. More."

He shook his head. "Nope. I'm tired out."

As the sky turned pink over the North Shore mountains, he threw a stick into the ocean for Susie to fetch.

"Are you going to live with us?" Cassie asked.

Susie swam back with the stick in her mouth. Even she was starting to look tired. "Just until Grandma gets better."

"Oh." Cassie kicked some sand.

He put a hand on her shoulder. "Come on. I'll race you to the truck." He deliberately let her win. Yup, she was definitely going to sleep tonight.

After putting Cassie to bed, he poured the leftover soup into a Tupperware container and placed it in the fridge. He'd watch a little television and call it a night.

He was just clicking through some programs when Marie came slowly down the stairs.

"I have something to discuss with you," she said.

"Sure. Cup of tea?"

"Love one."

He returned to the kitchen and made the tea. What did she want to talk to him about that had brought her all the way down the stairs? He put a few cookies on a plate and arranged everything onto a tray then flicked out the kitchen light and walked back to Marie.

She'd turned off the television. He put the tray on the coffee table and handed her a cup. "Careful, it's really hot."

"Thanks."

"You're welcome." He took a chair across from her. She looked pale, with dark circles under her eyes. The surgery had definitely taken a toll.

She managed a smile. "Thanks for being here."

"I wanted to be."

She tipped her head. "But you had to leave your business during the busiest season."

He shrugged. "Some things are more important than business."

Marie took a sip of tea then rested the cup on her knee. "I want to talk to you about Cassie."

"Sure. What's up?"

She shifted a little in the armchair. "I'd like you to take her home with you—just until I get better." She met his eyes. "I can't do it anymore. I want to, but I can't. I'm just too sick." She looked like she was about to cry.

Jake leaned forward. "Slow down now. It's OK." He made a play at humor. "This isn't about me letting her jump on the bed, is it?"

She smiled and shook her head. "No, it's not that. I've been thinking a lot about this . . . even before I went into the surgery. You know, if anything happens to me, I want Cassie to go to you. The lawyer said it would help if Cassie had actually lived with you. This is our opportunity to make that happen. I'll miss her, but it would be for the best."

"It's not a bad idea—except for one thing."

"What?"

"I'm not comfortable leaving you here."

Marie sighed. "But I can't go to Rosetown—not until I finish my treatments."

"I know, but you shouldn't be alone."

Marie glanced at a framed picture of Cassie on an end table. "I have friends and neighbors who will help out."

Jake leaned back, steepled his fingers, and tapped his chin. "And as soon as you're through treatment, you'll move to Rosetown?"

"Absolutely. Cassie can live with me, or we can work out something where she goes back and forth. She needs both of us. She's always telling her friends about you. I think it bothers her to be the only one in the kindergarten class being raised by a grandmother. Besides, she'll be finished school at the end of next week. It would be the perfect time to go."

He liked that Cassie talked about him when he wasn't there. "Does she ever mention her mother?"

Sadness crossed Marie's face. "Never."

This probably wasn't the best time to mention Maggie, but he needed to let Marie know. "I've met someone."

She placed her teacup on the table. "So maybe you don't want to be tied down with a child."

"No, that's not why I told you. I'd love to have Cassie. I just wanted you to know that there's someone in my life—someone I really care about."

Marie smiled. "I'm glad for you, Jake. I really am. Does she like children?"

Jake pictured Maggie outside the church, handing out candy to all the kids. "She does."

"That's wonderful. I hope I can meet her."

"It's early on. We'll see how it goes." His thoughts shifted to Cassie. It would be nice to be home, able to work. But how would he work with a six-year-old around? What did he know about having a child full time?" He'd wanted Cassie to live with them when he was with Jasmine, but to be a single dad . . . Could he do it?

Marie patted his leg, like she knew what he was thinking. "Of course, you'll have to line up a daycare. I wouldn't expect you not to work. Why don't you think about it for the night?" She rose slowly and grimaced.

She was in pain. Of course she couldn't be expected to look after an active six-year-old. Jake jumped up. "I don't need to think about it. I'd love to have her."

"Then it's settled." She took his arm for support.

"But I'm hiring a live-in caregiver to look after you, at least until you're steady on your feet."

She shook her head. "I don't need that."

"Then I'll stay here, and you'll have to put up with Cassie jumping on your bed."

Marie chuckled. "OK, Mr. Bossy . . . whatever you say." She glanced at his face. "You know, I think Cassie is going to be just fine living with you."

Chapter 14

ALL LITTLE GIRLS LIKED BUBBLES AND BUBBLE WANDS. AT least, Maggie hoped so, because that was what she'd brought for Cassie. She pulled into the gravel parking lot at Jake's house, cut the engine, and took a moment to gaze at the river. She felt all fluttery inside. She'd been surprised when Jake called to say he was returning after only two weeks, and even more surprised when he told her that Cassie was coming home with him.

As she walked up the driveway, the door opened, and Susie came bounding out. She reached down to pat the dog then looked up and saw Jake. Blue eyes, a day's growth of beard, and hair that needed trimming—she kind of liked the rugged look. She wanted to run into his arms, but instead she just quickened her pace. He stepped out to meet her, gave her a hug, and opened the door wide.

Cassie sat at the kitchen island with a bowl of cereal in front of her. She was wearing pajamas, and her curly black hair was all messed up. She had large brown eyes and a slightly upturned nose.

"Cassie, this is Maggie," Jake said.

Maggie smiled. "Hi."

Cassie's answering smile was just like Jake's—fascinating when there was no biological connection. "Hi. Are you my dad's girlfriend?"

"I'm his friend."

"Oh. Grandma said I would meet his girlfriend."

Maggie glanced at Jake. He turned around, reached for the coffeepot, and held it up. "Like some?"

"Sure." Maggie handed Cassie her gift. "Here's something for you."

"Bubbles!"

Jake kept his eyes on Cassie. "What do you say?"

"Thank you."

A silence seemed to hang over them.

"So . . ." Maggie finally said. "Are we still going for the picnic?" That sounded lame. They'd just discussed it on the phone.

"That's the plan." Jake smacked a bubble that hit him on the face. Cassie giggled. "OK, Miss Bubble, we're going to take you to the swimming hole."

Cassie looked intrigued. "How big is the hole?"

"It's big, like a little lake."

"Are there fish?"

"Might be."

"Is there seaweed?"

"No, it's not like the beach in Vancouver. It's not salt water. It's just a part of the river that decided to come in and make a swimming hole."

She grinned. "I've never swum in a hole before."

"First time for everything. Go get dressed. Put your swimsuit on under your clothes."

Cassie jumped down from the bar stool and grabbed Maggie's hand. "Do you want to see my room?"

"Sure." Maggie followed Cassie down the hallway. Other than a pink dog stuffy on the bed and a toy box in the corner, the room looked like an adult's room with its beige walls, green bedspread, and dark furniture. Cassie climbed up on the bed and started to jump. Susie barked.

Maggie didn't know much about children. Her whole experience with them consisted of a few babysitting jobs that she'd taken as a fourteen- and fifteen-year-old. What she did know was that Cassie had already forgotten her father's instruction to get dressed. "Where are your clothes?"

Cassie threw out her legs and landed on her behind then scrambled off the bed. She pulled open a dresser drawer and held up a T-shirt and a pair of shorts.

"And your bathing suit?"

After a long search, they finally found a red bathing suit stuffed in a side pocket of the suitcase in her closet.

"Would you like me to do your hair?"

Cassie nodded. She pulled a box of elastics and barrettes out of the top drawer. "Grandma uses these."

Jake wrapped up the chicken salad sandwiches. The barking had died down. What were they doing in the bedroom for all this time? He threw some apples and bottles of orange juice into the cooler, used a cloth to wipe the crumbs from the kitchen island, and headed down the hallway.

Cassie sat across from Maggie on the bed, her hair done in two fancy-looking braids. "Hi, Daddy," she said. She turned back to Maggie. "So I dug a big hole in the dirt and put her in it, and I saw this big beetle come over, and do you know what he said?"

"What?"

"He said . . ." Cassie changed her voice to a high squeaky beetle voice, "'I'm sad, because I can't live with you under the dirt, Dolores.'"

"What did Dolores say?" Maggie asked.

"She said, 'Harold, it's over. It's moist and dark in the dirt, and I'm not leaving again.'"

Maggie furrowed her brows. "So that was it. They broke up?"

Their expressions were so serious that Jake had to hold back a chuckle.

Cassie smiled. "Yup, they had to. Worms and beetles can't have babies or be a family."

"That's a sad story."

Cassie tipped her head from side to side as if to say maybe, maybe not. "They both got new families, and it was better that way." She lifted her hands and shrugged.

"And all this happened right in your own backyard?"

"Grandma's backyard."

"Wow!" Maggie turned and flashed Jake a smile that almost took his breath away. "Ready to head out?" she asked.

The swimming hole was where the river eddied into a pool. There were no currents, and a natural gravel sandbar prevented the swimmers from being pulled into the river's main stream. People were sitting on blankets. Children were swimming, splashing, and floating on inner tubes. Some were using a rope swing that extended out over the water.

Cassie and Maggie stripped down to their bathing suits, laid out the blanket, and sat down. Maggie leaned back and felt the stir of a breeze: it smelled like sage and sunscreen. She pulled her own sunscreen from the beach bag and rubbed it on herself then turned to Cassie, who sat beside her blowing bubbles. "Put out your arms. This will keep you from burning."

Jake arrived, having changed into his swimming trunks, and joined them. Maggie glanced at his firm bare chest and swallowed hard. She glanced down the beach, looking for a distraction. "See the blonde woman with the red hair band? That's Sandra. She runs a daycare at her home."

"Right. Sandra Baines," Jake said. "I know her husband. I'll talk to her later. I'm going for a swim. You coming, Cassie?"

They ran into the water, swam over to the other side, and climbed out. Jake grabbed the rope and pulled it toward them. It made her think of Tarzan and his child. He gave a few words of instruction and handed Cassie the rope. Cassie swung out like it was a jungle vine and dropped in with a splash. She really was Jake's daughter. She'd probably be challenging the rapids by the time she was fourteen.

Jake beckoned for Maggie to join them.

She ran into the cold water, front-crawled to the far side, and pulled herself out. When he put a hand on her waist and passed her the rope, she almost said, *You Tarzan, me Jane.* Instead she just gave a whoop, swung out, and let go. *Splash*—so exhilarating! No sooner had she emerged than Jake splashed in beside her. He pulled her toward him and kissed her lightly. "I really missed you."

"Me too," was all she could manage.

Cassie swam over, and they took turns throwing her back and forth as she giggled with pleasure. Then Jake put Cassie on his shoulders and let her dive off. He was a great father. *Jeepers.* If he didn't get custody, something was very wrong with the legal system.

At lunchtime, Jake took Cassie to meet Sandra. Unfortunately, Tamara Swift was in the group. As Jake approached, Tamara stretched out her long legs and arched her back to put her large bikini-clad breasts on full display. Her young son approached, and she batted him away like a fly. Jake nodded at Tamara but quickly turned to Sandra. Good—Maggie didn't like the thought of him being the least bit interested in anybody else—*especially* Tamara Swift.

When they returned, Maggie handed them each a sandwich. "How'd it go?"

"We're going over there on Thursday to see the daycare." He shook his head. "This is all so new to me." He glanced back at the group of women. "I'd rather have met a grizzly than faced that bunch."

Maggie smiled. The women were all leaning into a circle. "I think the gossip has already begun."

Jake sighed. "Let it."

After they finished eating, Cassie skipped over to where Sandra's son, Johnny, was shoveling pebbles into a bucket. She plopped down beside him and blew some bubbles.

Jake stretched out beside Maggie, his elbow down, his head propped on his hand. He reached out and touched her leg. "Looks like you've been working out."

"Jogging every day."

He stroked her leg and gave her an admiring scan from her eyes to her toes. Her pulse quickened, and she pulled out her cherry lip balm and moistened her lips. "Cassie seems like a great kid."

"A little rambunctious, but I like her that way."

She glanced over Jake's head. Tamara was staring, a predatory look on her face.

"Come to supper," he said.

Maggie turned her focus back to him. "Tonight?"

He glanced behind him to see what had been holding her attention. "Yes, but if you can't make it, I'm sure that Tamara would like to come."

She slapped his arm before she could think not to. "I thought you said you didn't like going over there."

Jake laughed. "Hey. Glenn told me that every guy in town was at the restaurant while I was away, eating steak and hoping to ask you out."

"Not just me. Lily too."

Now it was Jake's turn to frown. "Did you go out with anyone?"

Instead of answering, she just lay back on the blanket and tucked her hands behind her head. She gave him a coy smile. "Sure, I'd love to come to supper."

Chapter 15

MAGGIE PULLED SOME CLOTHES FROM THE DRYER WHILE Jeannie Brown, Bob's wife, stuffed two washing machines with dirty towels and sheets.

"So how are things going now that Jake has Cassie with him?" Jeannie asked.

"Not bad. We've been spending time together, but the competition's grown stiff. Seems like a lot of women are attracted to him."

Jeannie turned on the washing machines. "Time to make your big move, then."

"Pardon me?"

Jeannie turned to face her. "You know. When you want more."

Maggie's face grew warm. Was Jeannie, at sixty years of age, about to lecture her on how to seduce Jake? "Go on."

"All through high school, Bob and I were just friends. Then one day I saw Sally Thompson flirting with him, and I said to myself, 'Jeannie, it's time to make your move and make it now.'"

"So did you?"

"Absolutely. We were out at a concert with a group of friends, and I just took his hand."

"And?"

Jeannie's whole face lit up. "And the rest is history. We married, had our children, watched them grow up, immigrated to Canada, and bought this motel."

Maggie picked up her laundry basket. "So you just took his hand?"

"That's all."

"I'll keep that in mind. I've got to go to work."

Jeannie made a face. "Again?"

She shrugged. "Just for the lunch hour. I told you how angry Maynard was when he found out I'd used his personal steak supply, right?"

"Yes, but you said that he backed down when you showed him how much money you'd brought in."

"And now he wants to run the steak special every Tuesday, and he insists I be there."

Jeannie followed her outside. "I wish that Bob and I had time to come in."

"I could cook the special for you right here. How about tonight?"

"Really?"

"Sure. I'll invite Jake. You and Bob can meet Cassie."

"Wonderful. I'll bring the wine."

Thirty minutes later, Maggie slipped in through the back door of the restaurant. Kyle had the steaks out and was mixing up the marinade.

"Hey, Kyle."

"Hey."

"Where's Maynard?"

"Not in yet."

What was with Maynard these days? He came in late and left early. He should've given Kyle a raise for the way he'd been picking up the slack. She grabbed an apron and tied it around her waist.

Two new waitresses were working today. Unbelievable—Maynard hadn't even come in to train them.

She was placing an order on the pass-through, when Jake and Cassie strolled in. Cassie wore striped shorts, a flowered T-shirt, and gum boots. Her hair was pulled back under a red hair band. "You OK, Kyle?"

"Fine."

She walked out and Cassie ran over. "Hi, Maggie."

Jake smiled.

"You have the day off?" she asked.

"Yes. We were hoping you could come over."

"Jeannie and Bob are coming for supper. Join us."

"Sounds good."

She hurried back to the kitchen. "Sorry, Kyle."

"No problem."

The lunch crowd had almost cleared out when Maynard sauntered into the restaurant like he didn't have a care in the world.

Maggie frowned. "Could I talk to you for a moment?"

He lifted his brows.

She motioned that they should go to the front. Maynard tilted his head toward Deb and Jill, the new waitresses. "How are they working out?"

"Fine. It's Kyle."

He frowned. "Something wrong?"

"No, not at all. He works really hard. He can hold down the whole kitchen. It might be a good idea to give him a raise . . ."

Maynard held up a hand. "Done. Dollar an hour more sound good to you?"

"Yes." Deb walked by and stuck an order on the order wheel.

Maggie met Maynard's eyes. "I think we'd better get to work."

He chuckled and followed her into the kitchen.

Jake handed Maggie a bouquet of red roses. She was wearing a sundress, her hair a mass of curls, and her eyes more green than hazel in this light. He gave her a kiss on the cheek. She smelled fruity and sweet. He'd have kissed her with a little more passion if he wasn't holding his daughter's hand.

"Thanks. Come in." She pulled out a vase and poured in some water.

Cassie skipped in, wide-eyed. "Everything is little in here. Look! A little kitchen and a little living room."

"Kind of like living in a playhouse, isn't it?" Maggie showed Cassie the bedroom, the bathroom, and all the little kitchen cupboards and drawers. Jake glanced around. The place looked cozy with potted herbs lined up on the windowsill. If Maggie asked Cassie to move in, Cassie would do it in an instant. She loved little places. More importantly, she loved Maggie.

When they finished the tour, Maggie touched his arm. "Let's go outside."

One of the picnic tables had been set up with a red and white checkered cloth. Jeannie Brown walked over, and although she'd met Jake only a few times, she greeted him like an old friend. "So this is Cassie."

"Cassie, this is Mrs. Brown."

"Hi," Cassie said.

"Would you like to meet our pet pig?" Jeannie asked.

Cassie nodded.

Maggie placed the flowers on the table. "Just let me get my scraps, and you can feed him." She disappeared inside and came back out with a bucket. She gave it to Cassie. "I'd come, but I've got a few more things to do."

Behind the motel, a pig stood blinking in the sunlight.

Jake lifted Cassie up to the bottom rail of the wooden fence.

"Just pour the scraps out anywhere," Jeannie said.

Cassie dumped out the contents. Arnold pushed the vegetable trimmings out of the way and gobbled the burnt toast and marmalade first.

"Can we ride him?" Cassie asked.

"No, dear, but you can pet him."

Jake smiled. "I thought you were talking about a pot-bellied pig. This is a hog."

Jeannie laughed. "In more ways than one." The pig had devoured all the scraps and was snorting for more. "When Bob bought him at a farmer's market, Arnold was a sweet little thing, and we had to bottle feed him for a while. We had no idea he'd grow this large, but by that time we were attached, so here we are."

Cassie hopped down, and they started back.

"Are you going to the fair this weekend?" Jeannie asked.

"We are. You?"

"Bob and I never miss it—No matter how busy we are."

They reached the courtyard, and Cassie joined a group of children who were playing with squirt guns. She was instantly sprayed then gave chase to the boy who did it. Jake laughed. Tomorrow, he was going to buy the biggest power-soaker gun he could find and turn Cassie loose with it.

Maggie was placing some steaks on the barbecue. He walked over and put a hand on her waist. She looked up and smiled.

"Need any help?" he asked.

"If you wouldn't mind bringing out the salad and dressing. It's in the fridge."

Five minutes later, Bob joined them. They sat down, and Jeannie raised her glass. "To the cook."

"To the cook."

They clinked glasses.

Bob took a sip of wine. "How's the rafting business?"

Jake cut up Cassie's steak. "Steady. And seasonal, of course. I'd like to get some kind of tourism going in the fall and winter."

"What do you have in mind?"

"Ice-fishing, snow-shoeing, wildlife viewing—that type of thing."

Bob tilted his head. "What about accommodation?"

"Are you interested?"

"Absolutely. This motel could use a face-lift. A few winter customers would help pay for that. What do you think, Jeannie?"

Jeannie glanced at the courtyard. "I'd like to install a swimming pool."

They continued to talk companionably, the sun warm and the food delicious. For dessert, there was homemade cheesecake then coffee.

Maggie collected the dishes.

"Let me help," Jeannie said.

"No, you just sit and relax. You've been on your feet all day."

When Jake entered the kitchen, Maggie was putting things into the fridge. She turned, her eyes suddenly inviting.

He took a step closer. "I was thinking. When you go to trial, maybe I could go with you."

"What about Cassie?"

"She could visit Marie. I'd feel better if I were with you. It could be dangerous."

"I'll be under police protection twenty-four seven, but I appreciate the offer." Her lips flattened to a firm line and her chin tilted up.

"I get the feeling this is something you want to do on your own."

"It's something I have to do on my own. Carlo has a way of unnerving me—I need to know I can face him again and not fall apart."

"Want a tip?"

"Sure."

"He's going to try to catch your eye. Then he's going to smile. It's a way to get your guard down. Look straight at him, and don't let him faze you. Then punch him hard—with the truth."

"Where do you get this from?"

"I box."

"I'll keep that in mind."

He looked at the door. "Guess we'd better get out there."

She stood on tiptoe and kissed him. "I appreciate you trying to protect me."

If only she knew how much he wanted to protect her. The thought of a bad guy out there made him want to find Carlo and punch the bastard's lights out.

As they stepped outside, Maggie slipped her hand into his.

Wait a minute. Had she and Jeannie just shared a wink?

Chapter

16

CASSIE WAS BESIDE HERSELF WITH EXCITEMENT AS THEY began their journey upward on the Ferris wheel, the smell of popcorn, hotdogs, burgers and fried onions filling the air. Jake stretched his arm out behind his daughter and gave Maggie's pigtail a tug.

She glanced across the seat at him. "Brat!"

He laughed. He hadn't felt this happy in a long time. Next came the Octopus, and then the Zipper. By the time he'd finished these rides, Jake felt like he was about to lose his lunch. "I'm taking a break. You girls can keep going."

Maggie and Cassie got onto the Tilt-a-Whirl. Jake waved as the attendant snapped the safety bar over their legs. They looked like mother and daughter with their identical braids and matching white T-shirts. Jake sat at a picnic table, pulled out his phone, and snapped a few pictures.

Tamara Swift strolled over. "Hi, Jake."

"Hi."

She removed her sunglasses. "You've met Randy, haven't you?"

"Hi, Randy." Tamara's son was about Cassie's age. He had a dyed-green Mohawk.

"Hi," he answered sullenly.

Tamara sat down, smelling of strong perfume and cigarettes. "I have a light switch that isn't working. I was wondering if you could come by and fix it."

Jake would bet his last dollar that the light switch was in her bedroom. "Sorry, I don't do electrical jobs in the summer."

She ran her fingers over his forearm. "Would Cassie like to come over and play with Randy sometime?"

"I don't think so."

As Cassie and Maggie climbed off the ride, Jake rose to greet them.

Tamara stood beside him. "If you ever need me to help out with Cassie, just let me know."

Jake extended his arms, and Cassie jumped into them. "How was it?" he asked.

Cassie grinned. "Fun."

Maggie cautiously approached. "Hi, Tamara. How are you?"

Tamara put on her sunglasses. "Fine. I was just offering my services to Jake."

A shocked look fleeted across Maggie's face, and Jake had to clear his throat to keep from laughing.

The two children sat on the opposite side of the picnic table.

"Ouch!" Cassie yelled and smacked Randy.

"Hey, what's going on?" Jake asked.

Cassie's mouth formed a pout. "He pulled my pigtail!"

"That just means that he likes you."

Randy crossed his arms. "Does not."

Cassie frowned. "It hurt." She looked like she was about to hit him again.

Jake walked around the table. "No pulling hair, and no hitting. I want you to apologize to one another."

Cassie gave him a stubborn look. "But you pulled Maggie's pigtail, Daddy."

Busted. "Yes, I did." He turned to Maggie and said in his sincerest voice, "I'm sorry I pulled your hair." He turned back to Cassie. "Your turn."

"Sorry," she said.

Maggie came around the picnic table and took Jake's hand. He squeezed it then draped an arm over her shoulder.

Tamara frowned. "Come on, Randy. Let's go."

Jake was going to protest that Randy hadn't apologized, but thought better of it. Randy was her problem. He'd talk to Cassie about it later. Maybe even teach her to throw a good punch—just in case someone tried to bully her. This parenting business was getting more complicated by the minute. He glanced at Maggie.

She smiled. "You're a good dad."

Exactly what he needed to hear. "Thanks. Learning as I go. Hey, are you guys hungry?"

"I am," Maggie replied. "How about you, Cassie?"

Cassie, who was watching the crowd like she'd forgotten all about Randy, twisted in her seat. "Yeah!"

Jake took their orders and went to buy the food. When he returned, Cassie and Maggie each ate a hamburger and fries and drank a soda. Then they shared a bag of deep-fried mini doughnuts. Not only did they have similar tastes in rides, they apparently both had cast-iron stomachs. Jake drank a cup of coffee and ate a hot dog.

Lily and Rose strolled over. Cassie jumped up, and the two little girls hugged and danced around.

Lily smiled. "Hey, girlfriend. Hey, Jake."

Maggie motioned to the picnic table bench. "Join us."

Lily eyed the food wrappers. "No thanks. We ate already." Rose pulled on her mom's hand to whisper in her ear. Lily glanced their way. "Rose wants to know if Cassie could go on a few rides with us."

Rose pulled her mother's hand again. "She was also wondering if Cassie could come over for a sleepover."

Jake looked at Cassie. "Want to go?"

She jumped up and down. "Yeah. Yeah. Yeah!"

He tweaked her nose. "She'll have to borrow a pair of pajamas and a toothbrush."

"No problem."

Maggie elbowed Jake. He looked up. Mark and Gabriela were strolling across the grounds, their heads tipped together and arms linked.

"Well, well, well," said Lily. "The good pastor has found a girlfriend."

Jake expanded his chest. "I take credit."

Lily laughed. "Good work. You've succeeded where many others failed." She turned to Cassie and Rose. "You two ready for more rides?"

"She just ate," Jake warned.

"Don't worry, we'll do the tame rides first." If he knew Lily, the tame rides would be anything but. On the other hand, Cassie had already proven that she could take it—unlike her father.

After they left, Maggie took both his hands and pulled him to his feet. "What ride do you want to go on next?"

He groaned. "How about we play some games?"

They headed to the arcade, then, on Jake's request, went on the bumper cars. On the river he was brave, but on the rides he was a wimp. Fortunately, Maggie seemed to take it all in stride.

The sun had gone down when they finally left the fair. Jake threw an arm over Maggie's shoulder. "Ready to head home?"

"I am."

"My place?" He held his breath.

"Sure." She smiled, and his heart did a somersault.

Maggie sipped a glass of red wine. The French braids Cassie had talked her into felt too tight. She pulled out the elastic bands, undid the braids, and fluffed up her hair. Jake fiddled with the sound system in the corner until an Ed Sheeran song began to play. He extended his hand and pulled her up into a dance. She leaned into his chest, closed her eyes, and forgot about everything except him, her, and the music.

When he kissed her, she tacitly placed a hand on his muscular chest. He met her eyes, smiled, and continued to dance. A few songs later, they'd moved to the couch. A candle burned on the coffee table, a fire crackled in the fireplace . . . it was the perfect ending to a perfect day. He kissed her again. She ran her hands down his back and when he kissed her neck, she sighed involuntarily. He pulled back and looked into her eyes.

"Are you stopping?" she asked.

"Just checking."

She pulled him down on top of her, and her body went from embers to flame.

Then his cell phone buzzed. He groaned.

She laughed. "You have to get it. It could be Cassie."

But it wasn't Cassie. It was Chief Constable Frank Mackenzie. "Jake, I've got news," he said.

Jake was suddenly alert. "Yes."

"After you came in, I decided to do one more computer scan on Jasmine's ID. She's alive. She's living in Edmonton."

He gripped the phone as if crushing it would help him understand what Frank was saying. "You're sure."

"A few days ago, someone opened a bank account using her ID. At first I thought it was a case of stolen identity, but I just got the security video—it's her. Do you have your computer on?"

Jake grabbed his laptop and fired it up. "It's on."

"I'm sending it now."

He clicked on the email. The image was blurry but unmistakably Jasmine. "I've got it."

"She opened the account with a check for ten grand, made out to her by a Thomas Schmidt. Does that name mean anything to you?"

"That's her father."

"So she went home to her father?"

Jake ran a hand through his hair. "That doesn't make sense. He sexually abused her as a child."

"Any chance that she's being held against her will?"

"I don't know." He glanced at Maggie, who'd risen to her feet.

"She went into the bank alone," Frank said. "Doesn't mean someone wasn't outside threatening her in some way. I've requested that the Edmonton RCMP interview her."

"Why would she open an account now?"

"Probably figured we'd given up looking. I've got to go. Call you later."

Jake clicked off the phone and stared at it. This was good news. It had to be. So why did it feel so bad?

Because she'd left him. She'd let everyone think she was dead. Who does that?

"Jake?"

Maggie's face was white, her eyes wide. She stared at the image on the computer. "That's Jasmine?"

"She's in Edmonton with her father. She just opened a bank account in her own name."

"So how did she support herself until now?"

"Tom must have been giving her money, just to keep her off the radar."

"But why? This makes no sense."

"Nothing with Jasmine ever makes sense." Jake rose and began to pace. "I've got to call Marie."

Maggie went to the bathroom and splashed cold water on her face. Whether it was the fair food or what she'd just heard, her stomach lurched, and she turned to the toilet and vomited. She used some mouthwash and walked back out.

"Are you all right?" Jake asked.

No sense lying. "I feel sick."

"Me too." He shook his head as if he still couldn't believe it. "There's a slight chance that Jasmine's being held against her will, but somehow I don't think so. She left on her own that morning."

"Did you get in touch with Marie?"

"She's ecstatic. She'd convinced herself that Jasmine was dead."

"What about her being with Tom?"

"Marie can't explain it."

There were too many unanswered questions. Maggie already knew what he was thinking. "So when are you leaving?"

"As soon as I can figure out what to do with Cassie."

"I'll take her."

"You will?"

"Of course. There's no need to disrupt her world." It seemed like a crazy thing to say when Cassie's world had obviously just been turned upside down. "I mean there's no need to disrupt her world *yet*."

"Thanks." Jake walked over to the window and looked out. He turned to her. "Don't tell Cassie about this. Don't tell anyone. Not until I have some answers." A flash of awareness crossed his face. "I'm sorry about this . . . tonight."

"Don't be." A lump rose in her throat. She wasn't sure if she wanted to cry for Cassie, for Jake, or for herself. They were all threatened by this news when they should have been happy. It could have been a body that was found.

Jake hugged her. "I'll figure this out. I promise."

She fought for composure. "I know you will, but I've got to go home."

"Don't go. Stay for a while. Please." He kissed the side of her head.

She put her hands on his chest and took a step back. She needed to get away and think. "No, it's best I go. Call me in the morning."

Chapter 17

JAKE STOOD WITH A CRYING CASSIE IN THE FRONT YARD OF Lily and Ed's small, blue house.

"No Daddy, no. I want you to stay," Cassie sobbed.

Maggie hurried over. "Hey, Cassie, let's do something fun while your dad is away."

Cassie looked up. "What?"

"We'll go feed Arnold. Do you know what his favorite food is?"

"Toast?"

"Biscuits. Once I gave him some biscuits, and he started to nudge me like he was begging for more." Cassie stopped crying. "Plus, we could make cupcakes." She met Jake's eyes. He gave her a look that said *go for it, whatever it takes.* "Pineapple cupcakes, and we'll save some for your dad when he comes home."

Lily stepped out. "How about some breakfast?"

"Thanks, but I've got to get going," Jake said.

Maggie forced a smile. "Cassie and I can stay."

Lily turned. "Great. See you in there."

Jake gave Cassie a hug. "Go have fun."

Ed, who was sitting in a rocking chair on the porch, pushed himself up. "Come on, Cassie. Rose is waiting for you inside. Let's go wash up."

Once they were alone, Jake met Maggie's eyes. "I left a list on the counter. It's got Marie's number, Cassie's routines, how much to feed Susie . . ."

"We'll be fine," Maggie interrupted. "When will you get there?"

"If we leave now? Tomorrow morning."

"We?"

"Mark's going with me." He met her eyes. "I'll call you."

A wave of apprehension washed over her. Based on everything he'd told her, Jasmine could be dangerous. If backed into a corner, she just might demand her daughter back. "Jake, be careful."

He nodded, almost imperceptibly. "Don't worry. I know what's at stake." He gave her a hug.

As he drove away, Maggie felt a headache coming on. She opened her purse and swallowed an extra-strength Tylenol before entering the house.

Lily placed a platter of pancakes on the table. Ed sipped his coffee. The little girls chattered like chipmunks. Maggie forced herself to take a few bites of pancake.

Lily looked over. "You OK?"

"Just a headache."

Lily got up and poured Maggie a large glass of water. After they'd eaten, Rose and Cassie were excused and ran outside.

Ed pushed back his chair. "I'll keep an eye on them."

Lily picked up a chipped white percolator. "More coffee?"

"Sure."

Lily poured the coffee and pushed the cream toward her. "You have Cassie all day?"

"Maybe all week. I don't know." She met Lily's eyes. "I'd tell you if I could, but Jake asked me to not say anything."

"That's all right. I'm pretty sure this has something to do with Jasmine."

Maggie shrugged.

Lily smiled. "Don't worry. I'm not going to ask you anything more."

Jake and Mark took turns driving all day and most of the night. When they reached Edmonton, they pulled into a small motel. The plan was to get a few hours' sleep then stake out Tom's house. Mark collapsed on the bed and was snoring almost instantly. Jake drifted in and out of troubled dreams until the alarm on his cell phone sounded.

They headed to a nearby McDonald's for breakfast.

"Can you even see in those?" Jake asked, as he stared at his own reflection in Mark's mirrored sunglasses.

"Mostly." Mark took a bite of eggs. "So Marie doesn't know why Jasmine is here?"

"No. Why return to an abuser? It doesn't make sense."

"It's not as uncommon as you might think." Mark removed the sunglasses. "I've seen it before. I've met people whose entire childhoods are blank, especially the unlucky ones who were abused in the Indian residential schools. You should hear some of the stories that come out of the AA group. Memories can be so painful that they just get blocked."

"No memory?"

"No conscious memory. Sometimes when a person starts to deal with their addiction, it comes flooding back."

Jake put down his coffee. "Really?"

"Yes, but then they start to recover."

Jake took a bite of his breakfast burrito. Could Jasmine really not remember what had happened to her? He thought back to some of the things she'd told him. "Jasmine talked about her childhood almost like it was a fairy tale, and she was the princess."

Mark's expression was compassionate. "That's common too—creating an alternate reality to replace the one you want to deny. I didn't know Jasmine well, but even I could see she was troubled."

The restaurant was bustling with activity. People going about their normal lives. How many of them had to go spy on a spouse who'd let them think she was dead? Zero, was his wager. "I never should have married her."

"Then you wouldn't have Cassie."

"True." Cassie had always been the silver lining.

Mark sipped his coffee. "God works in mysterious ways."

"So He does." Jake gathered up the breakfast wrappers. "I guess we should get over there."

They parked a block away. An hour went by, then two hours. Jake got out and stretched his legs, then Mark got out, and finally, at three o'clock, a man came out of the house. Jake grabbed the binoculars off the seat. He'd seen pictures of Tom on social media—balding, overweight, in his fifties. It was him. Tom got into a white Ford van and drove away. Jake put down the binoculars. "Do you think she's in there?"

"Can't tell," Mark said.

Jake reached for the door handle. "I'm going to find out."

"You're going to knock?"

"Yeah. If she doesn't answer, I'm going in."

"Bad idea!" Mark had actually raised his voice.

"What if she's locked up?" Jake didn't think she was, but he needed to be certain. Maybe if she were being held against her will, he'd be less angry with her for leaving. "Call me if Tom comes back." He jumped out of the truck.

Jake rang the doorbell, knocked, waited then rang it some more. He walked around to the back of the house, where a high fence surrounded the yard. He picked up a patio stone and threw it against the basement window. He reached through the broken glass and undid the latch. No alarm sounded. *Thank God.*

He made his way upstairs. One bedroom was full of men's clothing, another was an office, and the third held women's clothes. It looked like Jasmine's stuff, but he couldn't be sure. He pulled open a dresser drawer—underwear, socks, and a photo of Cassie. She'd tucked her daughter away. Why?

His phone vibrated. "Yeah?"

"Get out. Now!" Mark said.

Jake raced to the basement. He crunched over the shards of glass, stepped up onto a chair, and crawled out the window. He exited through a gate that led to the lane and circled back to Mark.

Mark had moved to the driver's seat. "Get in."

"What's up?"

Mark started the engine. "Tom came home."

"Why are we leaving?"

"It's too nerve-wracking. What did you find out?"

"She lives there. Looks like she's there of her own free will."

Mark pulled into the same McDonald's they'd been at earlier. They ordered their food and sat at a table near the back. Jake's phone sounded. "Hello?"

"Jake, Frank MacKenzie here. Caught you at a bad time?"

"No. What's up?"

"The Edmonton RCMP went to Tom Schmidt's house yesterday. They interviewed Jasmine."

"And?"

"She said you were abusing her, and she feared for her life. That's why she chose to go into hiding."

"That's ridiculous. I never laid a hand on her."

"The officer asked if she would like to press charges. She declined."

Jake met Mark's eyes across the table. "She's insane."

"Jake, are you in Edmonton?"

"Got to go, Frank. Thanks for the info."

Jake clicked off the phone and updated Mark.

Mark held his hamburger suspended in mid-air and looked at the ceiling. "Oh Lord. The police know we're here, and I'm an accomplice."

"Don't worry. Frank didn't know about the break-in. Nothing was stolen. It will just look like a bungled burglary. Tom will think he scared the intruder away by coming home."

"But what if he reports it?"

"He won't. A new window is less than the deductible, and his premiums will go up if he tells the insurance people."

Mark shook his head. "You are *way* too practical for your own good."

Jake smiled. "Look, if what Marie says is true, Tom deserves it."

"I could debate that."

"Don't. What's done is done. Why would Jasmine say I abused her?"

Mark glanced out the window. "Maybe she felt cornered when the police showed up at her door." He turned back to Jake. "What do you think her next move will be?"

Jake took a sip of Coke and let his mind drift back to what he knew about Jasmine. "She may take off again."

Mark put down his half-eaten burger. "Which means we can go home."

"Or she may return to the house. So let's eat up and get back over there."

Mark put on the sunglasses and a baseball cap. "I'm beginning to regret this."

Jake laughed. "I was born for this."

"That's what I was afraid of."

Chapter 18

"Maggie. Maggie!"

It was a dream. No, it was a child calling. She opened her eyes. Cassie stood beside her. The clock radio said 2:00 a.m. "What's wrong, honey?"

"There's a crocodile by my bed, so I came in here."

Maggie flicked on the lamp. "Do you want to get in bed with me?"

Cassie nodded. She snuggled down under the covers and fell instantly asleep.

Maggie stared at the ceiling. Then it hit her. For a bedtime story, she'd read *Peter Pan*—and the ticking crocodile must have scared Cassie. She rolled on her side. Cassie had both arms around her pink dog stuffy. Poor kid. She had no idea of the forces at work in her life. Maggie pushed a wayward lock of hair off Cassie's face. "Night, night, sweetie," she whispered.

It seemed like Maggie had only just fallen back to sleep when Susie welcomed a new day by whining at the back door. Maggie put on her slippers, padded to the kitchen, and let the dog out. She was making coffee when Cassie got up. "Morning," Maggie said.

Cassie rubbed her eyes. "Morning."

"Did you have a nightmare last night?"

"No, I saw a crocodile in my room."

"How about we go take a look?"

Maggie pointed at a pile of Cassie's clothes lying on the floor. "Do you think that might have looked like a crocodile in the dark?"

"Yup, that's where it was."

"I used to think I saw things in my room when I was your age." Cassie looked up at her. "You did?"

"Sure, I thought I had a monster living under my bed."

Cassie giggled.

"Come on. Let's get dressed."

Cassie pulled on a pair of shorts and a T-shirt. "Can we go to swimming hole again?"

"No, you're going to Sandra's, and I'm going to work." Cassie looked disappointed. "But tonight, we can go to the motel and make Arnold some biscuits. Would you like that?"

Cassie clapped her hands. "Yeah! Then is Daddy coming home?"

"I'm not sure." Maggie grabbed the brush and some elastics off the dresser. "Let's do your hair."

Jake and Mark had spent a second day sitting in the truck watching the house with no sign of Jasmine. *Great.* His wife was alive but had obviously left again. Jake glanced at his watch. Five o'clock, and enough was enough. Tired and stiff, he opened the door. "I'm going to talk to Tom."

"I'll come with you," Mark said.

"No, you stay here. You can phone the police if anything goes wrong."

"What could go wrong?"

"He might try to kill me."

Mark paled.

"Just kidding. But I think it's better you watch from here."

Jake got out and walked to the house. He rapped on the door. Tom opened it. Up close, he had an unhealthy complexion and a fixed sneer. Jake came straight to the point. "I'm Jake Jones, Jasmine's husband."

"I know who you are."

"So Jasmine told you about me?"

Tom's eyes shifted. "I've seen pictures."

"Where is she?"

Tom used an index finger to slowly rub the side of his nose. "How would I know? She left after the police showed up."

Jake squared his shoulders. "She and I have some business to take care of."

Tom's eyes lit up with interest. "You mean with Cassie?"

Jake wanted to wipe the sneer off Tom's face with a fist, but that wasn't going to get him what he wanted. "Yes. Plus, half the house and business are hers. She'll want to talk to me."

Tom laughed. It took Jake aback. "What's so funny?"

Tom shook his head. "Mr. Cheapskate just got generous."

"You were giving her money?"

"What do you think? She sure couldn't live on the budget you had her on."

Shit. That's why Jasmine always had money to blow. He'd thought that Marie had been sending her funds to help out. His gut clenched. "I didn't realize that you two were back in touch all this time."

"You didn't realize a lot of things." Tom moistened his lips with his tongue. "By the way, if you see Marie, tell her I plan on meeting my granddaughter someday."

Jake straightened up—Mark called it his brick wall impersonation. "Cassie lives with me now. Come near her, and you'll be sorry."

"Sounds like a threat."

He nodded. "Believe me, it is."

Tom shrugged and closed the door.

When Maggie and Cassie arrived at the Ponderosa Motel, the first thing they heard was Bob's organ music blaring from the office. Cassie joined a group of children playing in the courtyard. Maggie stepped inside, opened up the windows, washed her hands, and took out some flour and baking soda. Keeping one eye on Cassie through the window, she preheated the oven and found her mixing bowl.

She called Cassie in, pulled over a kitchen chair, and motioned for Cassie to climb up. Maggie turned on the tap. "Wash your hands."

Cassie stirred, as Maggie added the ingredients. They rolled, cut, and placed the biscuits on a lightly greased pan. While the biscuits baked, they warmed up a can of beans. Maggie was too exhausted to cook anything else. After spending the previous day at the swimming hole with Lily and the two little girls, she'd come home and stayed up late talking to Jake on the phone. After hearing that he'd broken into the house, she'd grown even more concerned. He'd found out conclusively that Jasmine lived there of her own free will, but if he'd been a little more patient, the police would have told him the same thing.

Maggie washed a cucumber and gave Cassie a cutting board and a small, sharp knife. She handed her the cucumber. "Hold it with one hand and always cut away from yourself." Cassie, with an intense look of concentration, did as instructed.

They ate outside at a picnic table. People were barbecuing, some children were playing badminton and a few babies exhausted from the day were being rocked in their parent's weary arms.

"What did you do at daycare?" Maggie asked.

Cassie, who had been observing the flurry of activity, smiled. "We made ants on a log."

Maggie drew a blank. "What's that?"

"You take the celery, then you put in the peanut butter, then you put on the raisins."

"Ah, and then you eat it."

"Yeah." Cassie took a bite of beans. "Daddy makes good beans, too."

Maggie smiled. Cassie was easy to please. "Do you like the biscuits?"

Cassie nodded. She was such a sweet kid. If anything went wrong with this situation with Jasmine, and Cassie were exposed to Tom . . . Maggie pushed aside the thought. She had to stay positive.

After supper, they placed five small biscuits in a plastic container and headed around to the back of the motel. Maggie kept her cell phone handy just in case Jake called.

"Arnold, Arnold," Cassie called.

They could see the pig lying on his side in the garden shed. He lifted his head as they approached then rose and trotted over.

Maggie put a biscuit on Cassie's hand. "Hold your hand out flat."

Cassie reached through the fence and stood unflinching as the pig ate the biscuit. She smiled and fed him the remaining biscuits. Afterward, she climbed up on the bottom rail of the fence and leaned over to pat the pig's cheek. Arnold nuzzled and pushed at her hand with his nose. "He wants more," Cassie said.

Maggie laughed. "I told you he'd do that. He always wants more."

"That's all, Arnold. That's all. You liked those biscuits, didn't you? Yeah, you liked them lots."

Maggie's phone buzzed. "Hey, Jake."

"How are you?"

"OK. A little tired. Cassie's right here. Want to talk to her?"

"Sure."

Maggie handed the phone to Cassie. "It's your dad."

"Hi. Good . . . yeah . . . We're feeding Arnold." She giggled. "I will be. Bye, Daddy."

Maggie took the phone and glanced down at Cassie. She had to be careful to not mention Jasmine's name. "Any luck?"

"Nothing yet. I'll call you later once Cassie's out of earshot and we can talk."

"Sounds good."

"Thanks, Maggie."

"It's no problem. Cassie and I are having fun." Cassie smiled at the words. Maggie clicked off the phone. *Damn*. She'd hoped for some information. She put a hand on Cassie's shoulder. "Come on. Time to go."

They drove back to the house, Cassie humming, and Maggie lost in thought.

Cassie took a bath, put on her pajamas and brushed her teeth. Maggie was halfway through reading a bedtime story when she realized that Cassie had fallen asleep. She pulled up the covers, flicked out the light, and carefully stepped over Susie, who had positioned herself on the throw rug beside Cassie's bed.

Maggie moved to the living room and called Jake. "Hey, Jake. She's asleep."

"Good. How's she doing?"

"All right, but she crawled into bed with me last night. She thought there was a crocodile in her room. I'd read her *Peter Pan* before bed."

"I remember that story—a crocodile ate Captain Cook's hand. Who writes these kids' books anyway?"

Maggie smiled, but her curiosity about Jasmine kept her from commenting further. "So what happened today?"

"We watched the house all day. Jasmine didn't show up, so I knocked on the door and talked to Tom."

"And?"

"He said that Jasmine took off after the police questioned her. He knew who I was, and he said to tell Marie that he was going to meet his granddaughter."

"What did you say?"

"I said Cassie was living with me, and if he ever came near her, he'd be sorry."

Maggie got up and walked to the window. "So what's next?"

"Jasmine's not here, so we're coming home. Time for plan B."

"I hope plan B doesn't involve any more break-ins."

She could almost hear him smile. "I haven't thought it through. Hey, Maggie? I want to take you out when I get back—somewhere nice."

She couldn't resist teasing. "And by nice, do you mean the Golden Palace?"

He laughed. "No, I thought we could go to Lahara. But if your heart is set on Chinese . . ."

She cut him off. "Lahara sounds great." She smiled as she clicked off the phone.

Chapter 19

CASSIE PLACED HER FEET ON THE BOTTOM SHELF OF THE grocery cart, grabbed the handle bar, and took a ride. They loaded the cart with flour, baking powder, icing sugar, pineapple juice, food coloring, sprinkles, and maraschino cherries. At the cashier, Cassie helped load everything onto the conveyor belt.

Outside, a few clouds blew across the sky. A tumbleweed rolled down the street, and a train whistled. Although people walked by gazing at their cell phones, there was still a historic feel to this town. A few hitching posts remained, and Maggie could almost picture people tying their horses there.

When they arrived back to the house, Maggie left the doors open for the breeze to blow through and unpacked the groceries. Cassie dragged her toy box into the living room.

"Ready to make those cupcakes?" Maggie called out.

Cassie jumped up. "Yeah."

"Go wash up."

Maggie flicked on a country music station. They mixed up the batter and poured it into the cupcake tins.

"Grandma and I make cookies," Cassie said.

"What type of cookies?"

"Sugar cookies, chocolate chip." Cassie knit her brow. "And gingersnaps. Those are Grandma's favorites."

Maggie placed the cupcakes into the oven and set the timer. Cassie headed to the living room. As Maggie washed the bowls, beaters, and spoons, she thought how glad she'd be to have Jake home, even if things weren't resolved. All she'd done since he left was worry. She made a cup of tea and sat at the kitchen island to drink it.

In the living room, Cassie picked up her dog stuffy and made it hop across Susie's nose. Susie was the best-natured dog in the world. She was actually nudging Cassie's hands to play with her more.

The timer rang.

"Can we decorate them now?" Cassie called out.

Maggie took the cupcakes out of the oven. "Not until they cool. Come and help me make the icing."

They mixed up the butter, icing sugar, and pineapple juice then added yellow food coloring. Maggie opened the jar of maraschino cherries and the package of colorful sprinkles. She touched the cupcakes—cool enough. "We can decorate them now."

Cassie sat at the kitchen island and used a dull knife to spread the icing, shook on some sprinkles, and topped it all off with a cherry. The effect was a little lopsided, but this was a labor of love—they were for Jake.

They'd almost iced the entire dozen when Maggie heard the crunch of wheels on gravel. Susie barked and raced out. Cassie didn't appear to have heard anything, but that was fine. Let Jake surprise her.

As footsteps approached, Maggie glanced at Cassie, wanting to capture her expression when Jake walked in. But instead of joy and surprise, Cassie's face registered shock. Maggie whirled around. A woman stood at the open doorway. And although Maggie had only seen one blurry photo, she made the connection. *Jasmine.*

Jasmine wore a short skirt and a T-shirt. Her long blonde hair was held back by a pair of sunglasses. She tilted her head as if assessing the situation. "Hi, Cassie," she said.

Cassie stared, like she'd seen a ghost.

Jasmine opened her arms. "Come here."

Cassie climbed down, and a jolt of realization hit Maggie. She put a hand on Cassie's shoulder. "Stay put."

Cassie stopped.

Jasmine frowned. "Who are you?"

"I'm the babysitter." *As good an answer as any.*

Jasmine gave her a dismissive wave. "I'm Cassie's mother, so you can leave."

Maggie pulled Cassie close. "I wouldn't be comfortable doing that. Jake left me in charge."

"Jake's in Edmonton."

So Tom must have been talking to her. "I'm expecting him home any minute."

Unfazed, Jasmine strolled in and examined the cupcakes. She stuck her finger into the icing and licked it then crouched down in front of Cassie. "I missed you. Did you miss me?"

Cassie nodded, her face serious.

Jasmine rose. "So let's go for a drive. Just you and me."

Maggie stepped between them. "Leave, or I'll call the police."

Jasmine stood nose to nose. "She's my child."

Time to make the call. Maggie made a grab for her phone, and as she did, she heard the sound of running footsteps.

Jake stepped in.

"Daddy!" Cassie ran to him.

He picked her up and turned to Jasmine, his eyes steely, his jaw firm. "What's going on?"

"I'm sorry, Jakey. It's just that this . . . this babysitter was giving me such a hard time." She smiled and walked toward him. "I missed you."

He blocked her with an arm then passed Cassie to Maggie. "Could you take Cassie outside, please?"

Good idea. Maggie carried Cassie down to the patio below the deck. Susie, who'd followed them, rolled onto her back, and Cassie crouched down to rub the dog's stomach. With the deck door open above her, Maggie could hear everything that was being said.

Jake sounded furious. "You chose to let us think you were dead."

"That's your problem."

Jake lowered his voice. "Jasmine, did Tom help you leave that night?"

"Yes."

"He was here?"

"He was in Lahara. He was finally going to meet Cassie. It was just coincidence that you were such an asshole at about the same time."

"So you just walked up to the highway and met him?"

"No shit, Sherlock."

"And you'd take Cassie to him?" Maggie could hear the restraint in Jake's voice.

"Why not? He's my father, and he's been a hell of a lot better to me than you ever were."

"He abused you."

"Who told you that?" She sounded startled.

"Your mother did."

"She lied!" Jasmine yelled. "I've been with him for almost a year and he never touched me."

"Because you're a woman, and he likes little girls."

"You shut up, Jake. Shut up. Shut up. Shut up!" It sounded like she had both hands over her ears.

Maggie had heard enough. What would it do to Cassie if their argument moved outside? Time to get her out of here and return when things cooled down. She patted the back pocket of her jeans. No car keys. No phone. All she had to do was scoot in and get them. "Cassie, stay here. I'll be right back."

She jogged up the path and tiptoed in through the kitchen door, where she stopped short, unnoticed. Jake was holding Jasmine face-down on the living room floor. He yanked her arm up behind her back.

"Stop it. Stop it. You're hurting me!" Jasmine yelled.

He lowered his voice. "You're going to do exactly what I say."

"No!" She struggled.

He yanked her arm again. "Yes you are, and then you're going to get the hell out of our lives."

Maggie backed quietly out. No keys, no phone. She ran back to Cassie, her pulse pounding in her ears. "Come on. We're going."

"Where?" Cassie asked.

"To the church." Mark would be there. He'd know what to do. They ran to the dock. "Come, get into the boat. Quick!"

She helped Cassie in then hopped in herself. Susie barked. "Quiet, Susie!"

Jasmine screamed again. Good God, was he killing her? Maggie pressed the starter button, and the engine sputtered to life. Her mind started to buzz. Maybe Jake did have a violent side. Maybe he had abused Jasmine. She looked back. There was no one on the beach. As soon as they got around this bend, they'd be out of sight.

She reached under the seat and pulled out Cassie's life jacket. "Put it on."

It started to rain. Black clouds moved in. Thunder rumbled. Cassie gripped the seat as the boat began to buck over the waves. If they capsized, she'd have to grab Cassie quickly. "I want you to get down off the seat and scoot over in front of me." The bottom of the boat was filling up with water.

"It's wet down there," Cassie protested.

"Doesn't matter. I want you close." She helped Cassie make the move. A wave heaved the boat up and dropped it. The storm was picking up. This was a bad idea. She should have taken Cassie and just walked the mile down the road to the next house. "We'll be there soon." She wasn't sure if she was talking to herself or Cassie anymore.

There was a flash of lightning, and Maggie knew they needed to get off the water. She white-knuckled the tiller as they narrowly missed a jutting rock. The rain turned torrential, and Cassie started to shiver. Maggie looked up and saw the church. *Thank God.* She steered in. Mark was on the dock fiddling with his boat, which made a thudding sound as it smashed against the dock.

"Mark, what are you doing here? It's insane out."

He held up a piece of rigid foam. "Padding my boat." She threw him the rope. He caught it and pulled them in. "What are you doing?"

"We've got a situation back at the house."

Chapter 20

"ALL RIGHT, I'LL DO WHAT YOU SAY!" JASMINE SAID.

Jake let go of her arm. Jasmine scrambled to her feet and turned. "Asshole." She grabbed her purse and ran out into the pouring rain. Jake clutched his side and followed her.

"Cassie! Cassie!" she called into the wind.

So much for doing what he said. Maggie's car was here, so where were they? Jasmine ran down the path to the water. *Damn it.* Cassie didn't need to be confronted by her angry mother. Jasmine whirled around when she reached the beach. "You bastard. Where are they?"

Susie stood on the dock, her tail tucked between her legs.

Jake called the dog over before Jasmine noticed the missing boat. "Maybe they went for a walk."

She lifted a hand. "In this?"

He shrugged.

"She had no right!"

Jasmine got into her car, slammed the door, and drove away.

Jake walked up to the house and retrieved his industrial first aid kit from the hall cupboard. He went into the bathroom, pulled off his blood-soaked T-shirt, and threw it into the bathtub. The knife wound ran about ten centimeters in a diagonal pattern from his belly button to his hip. He needed stitches, but for now, some butterfly closures would have to do. He squirted on the alcohol solution, grimaced, and squeezed the wound together with one hand, applying the closures with the other. When the blood flow eased, he let out his breath and taped a piece of gauze over the whole thing.

Stupid. He should have seen it coming. Who grabs a purse and starts to rummage through it in the middle of an argument? He was lucky to be alive. He put on a clean T-shirt and a warm jacket to keep the shock from setting in. He walked to the kitchen and got out a plastic sandwich bag then picked up the bloodied knife and threw it in. Jasmine was no longer just the disturbed woman he'd been married to—she was insane. Thankfully, he knew exactly where Cassie and Maggie were: the next dock downstream was the church.

He got into the truck and shook the dizziness from his brain. Lightning flashed across the sky. *Shit.* Why the hell had Maggie taken the boat? He started the engine.

When he burst through the door, Cassie and Maggie were sitting on a pew, a wool blanket draped over their shoulders. Mark came out of the kitchen with a tray of steaming drinks.

Jake kneeled beside Cassie. "Are you all right?"

"Daddy, I bounced. I bounced lots."

He frowned and turned to Maggie. The thought that she could have killed both Cassie and herself infuriated him. "What were you thinking?"

She gave him an angry look. "Seriously? You're asking me that?"

"You should have waited outside. I was dealing with things."

"Right. You were definitely dealing with things." She turned her face away.

"Hot chocolate?" Mark asked.

"No thanks." Sirens wailed. *Great.* This situation was going from bad to worse. Two RCMP officers burst in—one male and one female.

"We've had a report of a child abduction," the male officer said.

Mark waved a hand toward Cassie. "The child in question is right here and perfectly safe."

The officer turned to Maggie and adjusted his holster. "Are you the babysitter?"

"Yes."

"Did you have permission to remove the child from the premises?"

"I gave her permission," Jake said.

The officer gave him a stern look. "I'm asking the babysitter."

Maggie frowned. "Jake asked me to take Cassie outside."

"Why did you bring her here?"

"To protect her."

The officer frowned. "From whom?"

Maggie glanced at Jake. "Her parents were arguing. She was getting upset."

The female officer came over. "I called the mother. She's on her way. I also called social services, and an emergency social worker will be here soon."

Jake glanced under his jacket. Blood was oozing through his T-shirt. The rain pounded the roof and daylight faded. The headlights of a car flashed through the windows, and the female officer stepped outside, re-entering minutes later with Jasmine.

Jasmine ran to Cassie. "There you are, sweetheart. Were you scared?" Cassie leaned against Maggie and didn't answer. Jasmine pointed at Maggie and turned to the male police officer. "She took my child without my permission."

The officer faced her square on. "The father says that he granted permission."

"He's not the father." She said it without blinking an eye.

Jake was about to open his mouth, but then realized that both these officers knew that Jasmine had been missing for months. Cassie climbed onto Maggie's lap, and Maggie folded her arms around her.

Ten minutes later, the social worker walked in. "I'm Anne Metcalfe," she stated. She wore jeans and a sweatshirt with a picture of a polar bear on the front. She had short gray hair, glasses, and there was something about her that said *you drag me away from home on a night like this, it had better be for a good reason.*

The female police officer took her aside. Anne nodded her head a few times then walked back to the group. "Who's neutral in this situation?"

"I am," Mark said.

"Please take the child somewhere soundproof in the building."

Mark reached for Cassie's hand, but Cassie wailed and wouldn't let go of Maggie.

"May I go with them?" Maggie asked.

"Who are you?"

"I'm a friend of Jake's—Maggie Jackson. I was babysitting for him while he was out of town. His wife, who'd been missing for ten months, came home and wanted to take Cassie. I wouldn't let her."

"I have custody," Jasmine screamed.

Anne lifted one hand. "Quiet! Until the child is removed from the sanctuary, there is to be no more discussion. Maggie and Mark will escort the child to a soundproof room."

Maggie pulled out a child-sized chair, and Cassie sat at the small Sunday school table. Mark found some paper and crayons.

"How about you draw a picture?" Maggie suggested.

"Of what?"

"Anything you like."

With Cassie occupied, Maggie signaled Mark that she wanted to talk privately. They walked over to a corner. "You know the social worker?" she asked.

"Yes. Anne is one of the best. She's been around for a long time. She'll do what's right for Cassie. You can count on it."

They stood there for what seemed like an eternity before they heard someone coming down the stairs.

Anne marched in and placed her hands on her hips. "Neither Jake nor Jasmine is going to get more than supervised access to Cassie. I've phoned the current babysitter, a Sandra Baines, and she's agreed to take her. Jake is coming in to explain." She walked out of the room.

Maggie's heart sank. Mark leaned in to her. "Listen, if Anne doesn't want Jasmine to have unsupervised access, then she has to apply the same to Jake. It's a good thing."

Anne re-entered the room with Jake. He knelt down, and Cassie held up her drawing.

"Look, Daddy. I made this for you."

He studied the picture. "I love it. I'll put it on the fridge." Emotions played across Jake's face. "Cassie, you know how you stay at Sandra's when I go to work?"

She nodded.

"Well, until your mom and I sort out some adult things, you're going to stay at Sandra's house."

Her eyes widened. "I have to sleep there?"

"Yes."

"I don't want to sleep there." She crossed her arms and frowned.

"I know, but this is one of those things that just has to happen."

Cassie met his eyes. "Then after my sleepover, I come home, right?"

"Yes, after your sleepover, which might be more than one night, you come home. Plus, Grandma is coming to visit."

Cassie's shoulders shuddered and she started to cry. "But I want to go home with you, Daddy."

Jake scooped her up and turned to Anne. "Let's go."

When they reached the sanctuary, Jasmine ran over. "You'll be all right, sweetheart. I'll come visit you."

Cassie turned her face into Jake's chest.

They walked out to the parking lot. The female police officer held the back door of the cruiser open. Jake placed Cassie in beside Anne. He crouched down and took her hands.

Tears ran down Cassie's cheeks. "No, Daddy, no. I want to come with you."

He kissed her on the side of the head and closed the door. The last thing Maggie saw was Cassie's small white face looking back at them.

Jasmine came out. "See you all in court." She got into her car and raced away.

Jake looked shattered. "I'll drive you back."

"Sure." What choice did Maggie have? It wasn't like she could take the boat back.

He drove in silence. Finally, he turned. "What happened before I came home?"

"I don't want to talk about it." She stared out the window and held back the tears.

"I just want to know why you took Cassie away. I asked you to take her outside, not risk her life."

"Look Jake, from now on she's your responsibility. I'm out."

He winced, as if her words had physically hurt him.

She bit her lip. She'd thought he was the good guy in the marriage. *Hah.* They were both insane.

At the house, Maggie quickly gathered her belongings and retrieved her purse from the living room. Jasmine's twisted and broken sunglasses lay under the coffee table.

Jake, pale and shell-shocked, was making tea in the kitchen. "Could we talk?" he asked.

She couldn't feel sorry for him—not after what she'd seen. She shook her head and walked out the door.

Chapter 21

JAKE RANG SANDRA'S DOORBELL AND GLANCED AT HIS wrist-watch. His scheduled visit with Cassie was set for three o'clock. Five minutes early. If social services didn't like it, too bad. Sandra opened the door, and Cassie launched herself into his arms. The doctor had just told him a few hours ago—no lifting. He glanced down and let out a breath. No blood seeping through his T-shirt. Thank God. The last thing he needed was for Cassie to learn he'd been injured. She'd been through enough already.

A woman with shoulder-length brown hair stepped forward and extended her hand. "I'm Eva Murray, the social worker."

Jake shook her hand.

"I'll take the other children outside so you and Cassie can be alone," Sandra said.

But they wouldn't be alone. Eva would be in the room. *Forget that.* "We'll go outside with you."

When they got out to the yard, he helped Cassie onto the tire swing and gave her a push.

Eva sat on a nearby lawn chair, probably judging his every move. *Let her.* Jasmine, who had barely given Cassie the time of day, now wanted to take her daughter to Edmonton. Surely if the authorities didn't believe she was unfit before, they'd believe it now. Jake had taken pictures of the knife wound and made a full police report on the incident. Still, Jasmine had a way of twisting information around to serve herself. The sooner this was over and he had Cassie back home, the better.

Jake spent most of the visit watching as Cassie ran around with her friends. He wanted to keep things as normal and comfortable as possible.

"How about a game of tag?" Sandra suggested when activity hit a lull. "Sam, you're it."

Cassie joined the game.

Sandra came over. "How are you?"

Eva was a short distance away, out of hearing range. "Holding up. How's Cassie making out?"

Sandra pushed back her blonde hair. "She cried herself to sleep last night. I wanted to let her call you, but you know . . . it's not allowed."

"Has her mom visited?"

"Her visit was at one." Sandra shook her head and kept her eyes on Eva. "It shouldn't be allowed. Cassie has no idea why Jasmine is back in her life. She's really uncomfortable. Sorry, I just had to vent."

"I forgot. Her favorite stuffy is in the truck."

Sandra nodded.

Jake opened the white picket gate.

"Daddy!" Cassie raced over.

Eva jumped up. "She cannot leave the yard!"

Jake glared. "I'm just getting something out of the truck." He took Cassie's hand and walked her back into the yard. "Stay here."

He could feel Eva's eyes on him as he opened the truck door. He grabbed the pink dog stuffy and took it to Cassie.

Cassie hugged it. "Doggy!"

"I couldn't bring Doggy to you last night. Tonight, if you feel sad, you hug Doggy and remember that I love you." He tussled her hair. "And guess what."

She looked up. "What?"

"Grandma is coming today. I'm picking her up at the airport."

"When?"

He managed to crouch without wincing. "Right after I leave here."

Cassie threw her arms around him. "And then I'm coming home?"

"Soon."

She pulled back, her lower lip trembling. "Daddy, I want to go home now."

He glanced at his watch—the hour was almost up. He didn't want it to end in tears.

Sandra strolled over. "Hey, Cassie, I was just going to make some chocolate chip cookies. Want to be my helper?"

Cassie glanced at Jake.

"Go on. I'll have one of those cookies tomorrow." He gave her another hug.

Sandra took the children into the house, and Jake headed out. He got into the truck and smacked the steering wheel but couldn't stop the flow of tears. Marie's plane landed in less than an hour. He took a gulp of air, started the engine, and headed to the Lahara airport.

Chapter 22

MAGGIE GAVE HER NAME AT THE RCMP RECEPTION DESK. Why had she been called to make a police report now? Four days had passed since Jasmine showed up. Maggie had said what she had to say at the church. Couldn't they just leave her alone and let her put the whole messy incident behind her?

A blonde police officer walked out and extended her hand. "I'm Constable Gray. Thanks for coming in." She escorted her to a room with a table and a few chairs and motioned for her to sit. She handed her a report form. "I'd like you to write down everything that took place on July twenty-second."

Maggie stared at the blank page. "I don't know where to begin."

"Chief MacKenzie wants to know every detail, from the time Jasmine arrived at the house until social services removed Cassie from the church."

"OK." She started to write. When she came to the part where she had re-entered the house, she stopped. What if reporting this caused Jake to lose custody? But if Jake hurt his wife, wasn't that his responsibility? She glanced at the bottom line where she would sign her name. Her own honesty was at stake. Look at what trying to protect Carlo had cost her. She wrote down everything exactly as it had happened.

"I'm finished," Maggie said.

Constable Gray walked over. "Sign and date it."

She signed and dated it, and Constable Gray added her name as the witness.

Maggie stepped out the door and put on her sunglasses against the brightness. It was her day off, and since she'd stopped seeing Jake, she didn't know what to do with herself. She was having difficulty reconciling the man she thought she knew with the guy who held his wife down on the floor. After all their conversations, how could Jake think such violence was acceptable? Still lost in her thoughts, she ran into Gabriela.

"Hi," Gabriela said. "What are you up to?"

Maggie shook her head, her stomach churning with anxiety. "I had to make a police report."

Gabriela touched her arm. "I heard that Jasmine was back in town. I was just going home to have lunch. Like to join me?"

"Sure." Anything to take her mind off what she'd just done.

"Do you have your car?"

Maggie pointed to the Plymouth a half block up.

As they drove, she told Gabriela about the incident with Jasmine. Gabriela nodded in sympathy.

Gabriela's house was painted turquoise with white trim. Maggie removed her sunglasses and stopped to admire the planter boxes on the front steps. "What are these flowers called?"

Gabriela leaned over and picked one of the small orange flowers. "They are the goldfish plant. They come from Mexico. I had my mother send me the seeds." She turned the key in the lock. "My children are away at camp. We have the house to ourselves."

The living room had a small white terrier lying in one of the chairs. The dog jumped down, and Gabriela picked it up. "Hello, Chico." She rubbed the dog's ears.

Maggie was drawn to a picture above the fireplace of two children holding hands, their backs to the artist, silhouetted against a vast sky of pink, purple, and navy swirls. "Did you paint this?"

Gabriela smiled. "Yes."

Maggie took a step closer. "It's beautiful. Do you sell your paintings?"

"I sell them online." She placed the dog on the floor. "Would you like to see my studio?"

Maggie followed Gabriela across the hall. An empty easel stood near the window. Various paintings hung on the walls—orange- and crimson-tipped flowers, cows with pleading eyes, and scenes from Mexican villages of girls in colorful dresses and boys in blue pants and white shirts.

"You're gifted."

Gabriela shrugged. "I'm lucky to earn my living doing what I love."

They made their way to the kitchen where Gabriela poured them each a glass of pink lemonade and made two chicken sandwiches. Chico sniffed the floor around her feet. Gabriela deliberately dropped a piece of chicken. "Whoops!" she exclaimed. The dog swallowed it whole and looked up for more.

They took their meal to the backyard, where a brick patio was set up with a table and chairs, and a grapevine growing over a trellis offered them shade.

"So Mark told you about Jasmine?" Maggie asked.

"No. I heard that from someone else. I am not speaking to Mark."

"What happened?" Maggie paused. "Sorry. You don't have to tell me." It sounded personal.

Gabriela shrugged. "It's OK. It was my forty-seventh birthday last week. Mark invited my children and me over for supper and cake. We went, and he wasn't there. We sat on the porch and waited for thirty minutes. When he didn't come home, we went to the Golden Palace for supper."

"Jeepers. That's lousy."

"He didn't call me until three days later. By that time, I wouldn't pick up the phone. I don't put up with this type of thing—not anymore. My first husband, I met him when he was on a trip to Mexico. He brought me here. Two kids later, he met someone else."

"And he left you?"

Gabriela shook her head. "No. I kicked him out. I painted my way through my divorce. I won't show you those paintings. They are dark, ugly paintings from a time when my world turned black. Then, one day, I was painting another dark picture—which, by the way, is not for sale." She chuckled. "And I noticed that in one corner, behind some hills, I had painted the small, glowing light of dawn."

"It gets better. That's what most divorced people say." Maggie took a sip of lemonade. "When was your birthday?"

"July twentieth."

Maggie counted backward. "Mark was in Edmonton that day. With Jake. They were spying on Jake's father-in-law, trying to find out if Jasmine was staying with him."

"Mark? *Spying*?"

"Yes, the whole nine yards." Maggie smiled, remembering Jake's description. "Mark was wearing mirrored sunglasses and a baseball cap. He took it very seriously."

Gabriela laughed. "I can't believe it."

"He must have forgotten all about his invitation."

Gabriela contemplated the garden. "I think he remembers now, because he calls me ten times a day." She picked up the pitcher of lemonade and refilled their glasses.

Maggie lifted her glass. "To being done with men."

"Yes! Down with men," Gabriela said, her accent heightening.

"I said *done*, but that works too."

Gabriela's cell phone sounded and she glanced at call display. "It's him."

"You want to take it?"

She snatched up the phone. "Hello." She met Maggie's eyes as a long explanation came from Mark. Maggie stood and signaled that she had to leave.

"Just a minute." Gabriela covered the receiver. "Stay. I'll be off in a minute."

"I have to go anyway. Thank you."

Gabriela rose and kissed her on both cheeks. "Thanks for coming."

Maggie smiled and let herself out the door.

Chapter

23

JAKE HELD THE ZODIAC'S TILLER FIRM AS THE BOAT LEAPT over the waves. He felt like something that had been ground up and spat out. He'd been up most of the night with Marie, who'd been staying with him all week and was inconsolable when Jasmine refused to take any of her calls. *Some reunion.* Cassie still cried herself to sleep every night. And Maggie? She was polite when he was in the restaurant, but if he attempted to have a conversation, she turned and walked away.

The raft up ahead held six women, all in their twenties. Half the crew were looking back at Glenn when they should have been looking forward. Glenn wasn't helping with his flirting and jokes. One more set of rapids, and Jake would go home and have a cold beer on the deck.

When the crew finally paddled up to the beach, Glenn hopped out, high-fiving each of the women as they got out. Jake pulled the Zodiac up beside the raft.

As they loaded the boats onto the trailer, two women walked over. One was a blonde, the other a brunette. "Hey, we're going to the bar," the blonde said. "Like to join us?"

Glenn grinned. "Sure."

She gave Jake a questioning look. He was about to decline when he thought about going home and facing Cassie's empty room. "Sounds good. What time?"

Jeannie opened the door. "I wouldn't let him put on his music. Come in."

Maggie stepped inside and handed her a bottle of white wine. "I thought it seemed quiet."

Bob, wearing a green flowered apron, came out of the kitchen. He was using a wooden spoon to stir some batter in a glass bowl. "Hi, Maggie, glad you could join us."

"Hi. Do you need any help?"

"No, no. You two just sit and relax." He disappeared into the kitchen, and a few minutes later, the organ music began.

Jeannie shook her head and poured them each a glass of wine. "So much for quiet. How was your day?"

Maggie took a sip. "OK."

"You don't seem yourself."

"I'm not. Ever since I made that police report, I feel guilty."

Jeannie tipped her head. "It's not your responsibility, love. That's a legal document. You had to tell the truth."

Maggie stared at her wine glass. "What if Jake loses custody? What if Jasmine takes Cassie to Tom? It will be my fault."

"The authorities aren't stupid. Jasmine abandoned her own child, and she sounds mentally unstable." Jeannie patted Maggie's hand. "Don't worry. It will all work out."

Maggie leaned back against the couch. "I don't know how I get it so wrong with men."

"You're talking about Carlo now?"

"Yes." Sometimes she felt guilty that Jeannie knew about Carlo when her own mother didn't. On the other hand, it was a relief that Jeannie finally knew why Maggie was there.

Bob stepped out and made an elegant bow. "Supper is served," he said in a posh accent.

They sat at the kitchen table, and Bob filled their plates with halibut, chips, and mushy green peas. Maggie poured on a little malt vinegar and added salt. The batter was crunchy and the fish flakey and flavorful. She dipped one of the homemade chips into ketchup. "This is delicious."

Bob smiled. "Thank you."

"Always good to marry a man who can cook," Jeannie said. She glanced at Bob. "Even if his choice of music is questionable."

Bob chuckled. "She seduced me, you know. Not the other way around."

Now *that* Maggie could believe.

Bob met Maggie's eyes. "So I hear you're leaving us in another month."

"Yes, I have to take care of some business." She was sure that Jeannie had told him all about Carlo.

"And it sounds like a nasty business at that."

She nodded.

Jeannie smiled. "I'm sure it will go fine, and you'll be back for a visit in the blink of an eye."

"I hope so."

"Ever thought about moving up this way?" Bob asked.

"Sure, but one thing at a time. Once the trial is over, I'll be able to figure out everything else." She frowned. "That is if Carlo doesn't get off on some kind of technicality."

Jeannie paled. "Then what?"

"Then I move to Africa, because there won't be any place on this continent I'll feel safe." She looked up. Jeannie and Bob had stopped eating. "Maybe we should talk about something else."

For dessert, there was raspberry trifle and a cup of black tea with cream and sugar. Bob brought out a deck of cards, and they played a few games of blackjack. It got Maggie's mind off the fact that she and Jake weren't speaking. She had this niggling feeling that somehow she'd got it wrong. But she'd seen what she'd seen. Jasmine had been helpless, and he'd been hurting her.

Maggie stifled a yawn. "I should get going."

She hugged them both and stepped outside. It was a warm night with a sky lit up by stars. A full moon cast a shadowy light across the courtyard. Funny, she was sure she had left her porch light on. She fumbled with her keys and stepped inside. She flicked on the light. Someone grabbed her from behind, putting a hand over her mouth and a gun to her head.

He pushed her down onto a kitchen chair. "Hello, Maggie."

Carlo. He wore a tailored shirt, his curly brown hair longer than she remembered. Her heart pounded, and she wanted to run, but the door was firmly closed behind her. "How'd you find me?"

"Luck." He reached into his shirt pocket and threw a piece of paper at her.

It was a newspaper article featuring a picture of Lily and Rose. Behind them, Maggie was lifting some food off the pass-through. She scanned the words—Chef Maggie Jackson's steak special. The travel writer must have asked someone her name.

He sat in a chair opposite her and put a hand on her leg. "I want the jewelry back."

She tried not to flinch. "It was a gift."

He smiled. "No gifts for traitors. Where is it?"

"Why should I tell you?"

He leaned forward, his minty breath in her face. "Difference between a quick and painful death."

Oh, God. He really was going to kill her. The fear rose from her belly to her chest. So much for bravery. "Please, Carlo. We can work this out. I'll lie in court. You and I, we had something. Maybe we could have something again. Maybe we could just disappear—together."

"Sorry, baby, you already got me arrested. They've closed down my restaurant and frozen my assets. When their key witness doesn't show, I'll be getting it all back."

She could scream. People in the motel would hear.

She glanced at the gun.

And innocent people would get shot. "Carlo, don't do this."

He pushed the gun against the side of her head. "Where is the jewelry?"

"I'm not telling." As long as she had something he wanted, he wouldn't kill her—she hoped.

Carlo jumped up, opened a kitchen drawer, and pulled out a butcher knife. He grabbed her hair then shoved her head down onto the table. He picked up the knife and wacked off a chunk of hair. "Next, it's a finger."

"I left it in Vancouver!"

He raised the knife again. "Liar. We searched your apartment."

"It's in Vancouver. I swear!"

"Where?"

"Outside the balcony doors. On that little ledge that overhangs the deck. I was afraid someone might break in and steal it."

He grabbed a handful of hair and yanked her head up. "So every time you wanted to wear it, you went outside?"

"Yes!"

It registered on his face that she was telling the truth. He sighed and glanced at his watch. "The pilot is waiting. Nice guy. For fifteen grand, he even put the rental car in his name. I'll be back in Vancouver to check in with pretrial services in the morning, and no one will even know that I was gone." He examined her for a minute. "Still letting your hair run wild, I see."

She self-consciously touched her curls, before she remembered that she wasn't that person anymore.

Rage. It was so much better than fear. It cleared her head, and she thought about possible weapons.

"Carlo, I have to go to the bathroom."

"I'll take that as your last request."

Carlo leaned his back against the open door while Maggie sat on the toilet and forced herself to pee. She scanned the bathroom. The nail scissors were still lying on the counter. She got up, flushed the toilet, and glanced in the mirror. He was looking toward the bedroom, gun at his side. She turned on the tap then carefully scooped the scissors and slipped them into the front pocket of her jeans. He turned around, and she pretended to be drying her hands.

Carlo kept the gun pointed at her as she came out. The bedroom was a mess. He'd emptied the closet and all the drawers looking for the jewelry. He grabbed her sweat jacket off the floor. "Put it on. Time for a drive."

Of course. He wouldn't kill her here. He'd take her out to the bush. She might never be found. She had to break away before she got into the car. If she could make it, she knew the area across the road like the back of her hand.

Rabbits zig-zagged to avoid a fox. Maybe he'd miss the shot if she became a rabbit.

The bar was full of rowdy merry-makers. Glenn was dancing with the whole crew of women, all of them laughing and tipsy after their day on the river. A good-looking redhead beckoned Jake to join them. He shook his head. Who did Maggie think she was anyway? Taking Cassie out on the boat. What would have happened if she hadn't taken Cassie to the church? If she'd been outside where she was supposed to be? Jasmine wouldn't have called the police. Social services wouldn't have become involved. Cassie could be home in her own bed.

He picked up his phone and pressed the speed dial for Maggie, but it went straight to voice mail. She was still ignoring him. He gulped the last of his beer before standing. If Maggie wasn't going to answer, she could damn well explain herself in person. He walked out of the bar.

Chapter 24

AS JAKE PULLED INTO THE PONDEROSA MOTEL, HIS headlights lit up two figures—Maggie and a Latino-looking man. She looked up, saw the truck, and glanced away. Her posture was tense, poised for flight, but she wasn't running. It had to be Carlo, and Jake would bet his last dollar that he had a gun tucked up under her jacket. He squinted his eyes. One wrong move and Carlo would pull the trigger. His stomach clenched, and he knew what he had to do.

He got out and whistled in a relaxed manner. "Hey, decent motel?" he asked.

"Sure," Carlo said.

Maggie kept her face neutral, but he could see the pleading in her eyes.

Everything in him wanted to reassure her. Instead, he nodded and strolled into the office. "Hi, Alexa."

"Hey, Jake."

"What's happening between Maggie and the man outside?"

Alexa glanced out. "He's looking this way. What's going on?"

"He's got a gun."

Alexa's face turned white. "Should I call the police?"

"Not yet. Just act like you're booking me a room." With a shaky hand, she reached for the registration paper and slid it across the counter.

Jake picked up the pen and jotted down the name, Carlo Romero, the car's description, and the license plate number. "As soon as I leave, call the police. Tell them he's armed, he has Maggie, and he's planning to kill her. What are they doing now?"

"He's pushing her into the car. God, she looks terrified!"

"Alexa, look at me." She met his eyes. "You can't let him know we're onto him."

"Right." She turned around and took a key off the wall. "Enjoy your stay . . . And they're gone."

Jake sprinted to the truck, turned on the engine and left off the headlights. He turned onto Ponderosa Drive, bumped over the rails of the cattle guard, and speed-dialed Frank MacKenzie."

"What's Carlo Romero got to do with her?" Frank asked.

"Ex-boyfriend. She was scheduled to testify against him."

"Where are they now?"

"Downtown . . . Wait—they're exiting north on the highway."

"Stay on them. I'm calling for back-up from Lahara and Pinton."

Jake threw his phone on the seat and kept his foot light on the gas pedal. He followed, their taillights blinking in and out of view. If he risked getting too close, Carlo might kill her on the spot. But if he didn't see where they turned off . . . he couldn't even think about that.

He navigated the twisty highway with only the moon to light his way. Every part of his body was tensed. He glanced at his watch. They'd been driving for thirty minutes. Where the hell was Carlo taking her? He licked his lips and answered his own question: any forested area where a shot wouldn't be heard and a body wouldn't be found. Ten minutes later, the SUV turned.

He reached for his phone.

"Yeah?" Frank answered.

"They just exited onto Brantford Road."

"Perfect. We can access that road from the other end. We'll set up an ambush at the decoy buck, but you've got to get him off the road—close enough for the officers to take out the tires."

"Can't they just shoot him?"

"Not unless he raises his weapon."

"Hey, Frank—" *Damn.* His cell phone had just gone out of range.

Maggie glanced in the side mirror. No sign of anyone. Jake wasn't following, but he would have called the police. When she'd seen him, she knew not to risk breaking away. Jake would have a plan. He wouldn't let her die. She needed to hold onto that thought, or the fear would consume her.

They'd turned off the highway, and the road looked familiar—it was where Lily had taken her to see the fake deer. She pulled the nail scissors out of her pocket and clasped them in both hands. She willed Carlo to keep driving, because as soon as he stopped, she was going to stab him, and nail scissors were no match for a gun.

She glanced in the mirror again. Jake's truck! *Thank God.* It was barely visible in the light of the moon. No headlights. Gathering speed. The roar of an engine. Then, suddenly, his high beams flooded the SUV.

"Son of a bitch! Who is that?" Carlo yelled.

Jake pulled up beside them. Maggie met his eyes. He nodded and slammed the truck into the SUV. *Bam.* He slammed them again. Carlo pointed the gun at Jake. The whole car was shaking as Maggie rammed the nail scissors into Carlo's arm. The shot went through their windshield. *Bam.* They were slammed again.

The car bumped over a meadow. Jake rammed them from behind. The headlights lit up the decoy deer. It stared at them with lifeless eyes just before they crashed into its side.

Maggie shook the fog from her head, slid across the seat, and got out. Pain shot through one leg. She staggered and turned. Carlo got out and raised his gun. A hail of bullets sounded, and he fell to the ground.

Police officers. Just in time.

Jake grabbed her by the shoulders. "Maggie, are you OK?"

"I don't think so." She collapsed into his arms.

Chapter 25

MAGGIE SAT IN HER BED AT THE LAHARA HOSPITAL, TRYING to clear her head. The medical chart hanging on the wall said she had a Grade 2 concussion, a sprained ankle, and bruises all over her body. Jake had saved her life, but he'd almost killed her in doing so.

A knock sounded on the door. Jake entered and pulled over a chair.

Maggie winced as she turned toward him. It all seemed a blur. The whole scenario played in her mind like a movie that she'd watched eons ago and couldn't quite remember. She did remember Carlo taking aim. And she remembered watching him die.

"If you hadn't come by that night, he would have killed me," she said.

Jake took her hand. "I know. Unfortunately, I had to get his car over to the blind where the police were hiding."

"Where's Cassie?"

"She's still staying with Sandra."

Maggie tried to shake the cobwebs from her brain. "Oh, right. Why don't I know that?"

"The concussion. There's still some swelling."

She touched the side of her head. So lumpy. "Is there a mirror anywhere?"

"Believe me, you don't want to look."

Jake looked good. She was angry at him, but she couldn't for the life of her remember why. "So I'm not going to win a beauty contest?"

He shook his head and tenderly touched her hair. "Not today. What happened?"

She reached up. Some hair was missing. She remembered Carlo and the butcher knife slamming down. She started to shake like she'd been dipped into an ice bath. Jake pulled the call cord.

The nurse hurried in and took her pulse. "Are you in pain?"

Maggie couldn't find her voice.

"I may have said something to set her off," Jake said.

The nurse pulled out a tablet. "Maggie, open your mouth. I'm going to put this under your tongue. It will help."

She opened her mouth.

"Just rest now," the nurse said.

As she drifted off to sleep, she was vaguely aware that Jake was holding her hand.

When she woke up, the nurse helped her to the bathroom then helped her to wash her face and brush her hair. "There's a police officer here to see you," she said.

Maggie nodded, and the nurse exited.

A few minutes later, Chief Constable Frank MacKenzie entered the room. He was wearing his full police uniform, his hat tucked under his arm. "Your parents and brother are here."

"Really?"

"Of course. I called Officer Sheraton in Vancouver. He says you fulfilled your duty when you agreed to testify. Now that Romero is dead, you're a free woman. Officer Sheraton called your family."

"Where are they?"

"In the hospital lounge, just down the hall. But before I go . . ." He handed her a business card.

"What is it?"

"The name of a psychologist in Rosetown. If you move back to Vancouver, you can see any registered psychologist. All you have to do is show the police report. Counseling is free for crime victims."

"I'll be fine."

Chief MacKenzie frowned. "Maggie, every officer on duty that night will talk to a counselor. It's never easy to kill someone or see someone killed, not even in the line of duty."

She glanced at the card. *Beatrice Jefferson, Registered Psychologist.* "I'll think about it."

"Good. Now, there are some people who are champing at the bit to see you. Shall I get them?"

"Yes, please."

Her family rushed in. Maggie reached out a hand. Her mother hugged her.

"Ouch, that hurts," Maggie said.

Her mother released her, and her father and brother both hugged her—gently.

Her mother eyed her up and down as if trying to convince herself that her daughter was really all right. "We came as soon as we heard the news."

Seeing her family again . . . It was just too much. Maggie burst into tears. Her father put his arm around her.

Her mother handed her a tissue. "It was terrible for you. It's over now. I'm so glad that it's over."

"Do you want to talk about it?" her father asked.

Maggie filled them in on what had happened, from the time that Carlo had shown up until the time he was killed.

Her mother pulled her chair close to the bed. "We were so worried about you when Officer Sheraton called and told us you'd gone into hiding. Such a gruff man. He barely answered any of our questions. We didn't even know that you were dating anyone, let alone someone who was involved in the drug trade."

"I knew," Rob said. "At least about the dating part. I met him on my last trip to Vancouver, but she swore me to secrecy."

"Why?" her father asked.

"Because he was forty-three years old." Rob placed his hands on his hips. "I told you that I didn't like him."

She crossed her arms. "But you don't like any of my boyfriends."

Rob shrugged. "True, but I especially didn't like that one."

A knock sounded. Jake stood in the open doorway with a bouquet of flowers. "I'm sorry. Am I interrupting?"

Perfect timing. "Not at all. Come in. Jake, these are my parents, Karen and Ray, and this is my brother, Rob. All three of her family members rose to shake his hand. Rob left the room and returned with another chair. Soon they were bombarding Jake with questions about his role in everything. Jake looked relaxed under their rapid-fire interrogation. He told them what a trooper she'd been, and how she'd kept Carlo from killing him, armed with nothing more than a pair of nail scissors. Her mother paled at this. He credited Frank MacKenzie and the RCMP with the whole rescue operation, even though they all knew it wouldn't have happened without Jake's quick thinking. When her family turned back to her with approval written all over their faces, Jake met her eyes and winked. She tried to hold back her grin.

"Mark has been asking about you," Jake said.

"How is he?"

"He's got a personal crisis on his hands."

"With Gabriela?"

Jake nodded. "Yup. He stood her up. To get out of the doghouse, he had to agree to take Spanish dance lessons."

"Does he like dancing?"

Jake crossed his legs, clasping his knee in his hands. "Don't know, but he'd better learn to like it—fast."

Maggie turned to her mother. "Mark is our pastor."

"Sounds like he belongs in the doghouse," Karen said matter-of-factly.

Jake laughed. "He probably does, but he was helping me out. I feel partially responsible. I've got to get going. My visit with Cassie is at three, and I need to go by work before then. He put the flowers on the end table and turned to her family. "Nice meeting you."

After he left, her mother found a vase, filled it with water and arranged the flowers. "Who's Cassie?"

"His stepdaughter." Maggie filled them in on the whole situation. As she did, she was hit again with the image of Jake holding Jasmine down on the floor. She decided to leave that part out.

Rob frowned. "I still don't get why you took Cassie to the church. Shouldn't you just have stayed outside?"

"I was scared that their argument would be too much for Cassie to handle." She raised her hands. "Doesn't matter now. What's done is done."

"His wife sounds terrible," her father said. "He won't get back together with her, will he?"

"Never."

A concerned look crossed his face. "You should steer clear either way, until things are settled."

"I will." It felt wonderful to be treated like a child again.

Her mother pushed a strand of hair off her face. "And when are you moving to Calgary?"

Well, maybe not *that* wonderful. "I'm not. I'll move back to Vancouver."

"Oh no. That's not a good idea. You need to come home after all this."

Ray shot his wife a warning look. "I hope that we can see Jake again before we leave. I'd like to take him out to supper. Repay him in some way."

Maggie sighed. "Plus, I need to pay him for his truck repairs."

Rob looked aghast. "You wrecked his truck?"

Maggie turned painfully to face him. "What is it with you guys and your trucks, anyway?"

"What kind of truck is it?"

"How would I know? It's a big black truck."

Rob rolled his eyes.

A nurse stepped into the room.

"We should get going," her mother said. "We'll come by and see you later."

Chapter
26

WHEN JAKE ENTERED THE ROOM, MAGGIE WAS STANDING AT the window, looking at the street below. She still had that crazy lopsided haircut, but he wasn't going to mention it. He cleared his throat. When she turned, her eyes went directly to the paper bag in his one hand and the tray of coffees in the other. "Is that real food?"

She sat on the bed, and he handed her a corned beef sandwich. "So your family left?"

"Yes. They had to get back to work. My parents are coming for a visit in three weeks. They were going to take a trip to San Francisco, but they decided they'd like to see Rosetown instead."

"You're not going back to Vancouver?"

"Not right away." She pointed to the Tensor bandage on her ankle. "I mean, can you really see me looking for employment like this?"

He unwrapped the second sandwich. She still had a cracked lip, a bruised cheek, and a cut over one eyebrow. "You look better."

She gave him a sideways glance. "Liar. I look awful."

"Let's just say that you look a lot better than you did."

She poured a creamer into the coffee. "I guess. How about you. Any injuries?"

Time to get things out into the open. He lifted his T-shirt. It was the first day he'd been able to leave the bandage off his wound.

Her eyes widened. "I'm sorry."

"It wasn't from the other night."

She looked alarmed. "When?"

"Jasmine did it. During our argument. She came at me with a switchblade. I disarmed her, but not before she nicked me."

Her eyes filled with tears. "Jake, that is more than a nick. Why didn't you tell me?"

He shrugged. "You didn't want to talk to me."

"Because I thought you were beating her up."

"What?"

"I went back into the house to get my keys and phone. Cassie was upset. I wanted to get her away and call you later. You had Jasmine down on the floor. She was screaming that you were hurting her."

Shit. If she'd seen that, no wonder she'd been ignoring him. "Sorry. I don't play nice when someone tries to kill me."

Her shoulders slumped. "I didn't know she'd attacked you."

Jake leaned back and took a sip of coffee. "So that's why you took Cassie on the boat. You thought I was roughing Jasmine up—using brute force to get my own way."

She bit her lip, her brows coming together. "Something like that."

"That's not how I operate. I thought you knew that."

"I thought I did too, but I got scared. Wait a minute—why did you come to the motel the other night?"

Busted. He might as well tell the truth. "I came to tell you off."

"Because I took Cassie on the boat?"

"Correct. I couldn't understand why you didn't wait outside. You do know that the worst place to be in a lightning storm is on the water."

"I know that, but the storm hadn't come up when we left. Are you still angry?"

He hadn't been angry since he'd seen Carlo with a gun tucked under her jacket. In fact, he'd felt quite the opposite. "Not anymore. Are you?"

"No. I don't play nice either when someone tries to kill me." She straightened her back and took a sip of coffee.

"The nail scissors?"

She tipped her head. "Hey, I saved your life with those. But I'm not sure my mother needed to hear about it."

He laughed and moved his chair closer. "We're quite the team."

She placed a hand on her bruised cheek. "A battered-up team, I'd say."

He got up and moved to the edge of the bed. She leaned against him. He put his arm around her and glanced around the sterile room. "When do you get out of this joint, anyway?"

She smiled. "Tomorrow."

"Need a ride?"

"I do. Did you get the truck fixed?"

"It's in the shop. I have a courtesy car."

"I'm paying the repair bill."

He gave her another squeeze. "Don't worry about it. I have collision insurance."

"That's covered?"

"Apparently."

She moved back and met his eyes. "I can't believe that Carlo is dead."

"I can't believe you dated him." *Oops.* He hadn't meant to say that out loud.

She crossed her arms. "Hey. Look who's talking."

He chuckled. "I get it. So let's make better choices."

"Let's." And she burst into tears.

First she'd been teasing. Now she was crying. "What's wrong?"

"I don't know. My emotions are all over the map. It's like everything is catching up to me."

"Hey, it's going to be all right. You've been through a lot."

She wiped away the tears. "Did you bring any more sandwiches?" She looked like a child asking for more ice cream.

He smiled. "Sorry. Tomorrow, I'll take you out for a real meal on our way home."

Chapter 27

BOB JUMPED UP FROM HIS PLACE BEHIND THE COUNTER. "Maggie! What a sight for sore eyes. Jeannie is going to be over the moon to see you. Jeannie—Jeannie!" he yelled through the door to the manager's unit.

Jeannie came at a jog. "What is it? She stopped dead in her tracks then ran over and gave Maggie a hug. "We were so worried about you. Thank goodness you're all right." She glanced at the Tensor bandage. "Is it sprained?"

"Yes, but I can limp. I left my keys inside the unit."

"Let me walk you over with some fresh towels."

Bob handed Jeannie a key. "You ladies take your time."

The courtyard was full of playing children. The adults were hauling coolers out to their cars, and others were heading to the office to check out. It all seemed so normal—like she hadn't been led through this same courtyard at gunpoint just four days earlier.

They reached the porch, and Maggie froze. Jeannie looked back. "I'll just go in first, shall I?"

Maggie inhaled and forced herself to take a step. Inside, all the clothes that Carlo had dumped on the floor had been put away, and the kitchen table was empty. Jeannie took the towels into the bathroom.

Maggie sank onto a kitchen chair. "There was a knife and some hair."

Jeannie came out of the bathroom. "I threw them out."

Maggie touched the side of her head. "He did this."

"That man was a brute."

"He said it would be a finger next."

Jeannie shook her head. "What did he want?"

"Some jewelry that he'd given me." She could almost feel her forehead being knocked against the table.

Jeannie gently touched her shoulder. "Did you give it to him?"

"No, I'd left it in my Vancouver apartment, but he thought it was here. That's why he tore the place apart."

"How about I make us some coffee?"

"Thanks."

Jeannie filled the pot with water and turned on the coffeemaker. "I hate to think what would have happened if Jake hadn't come by when he did."

"Me too." She twisted in her chair. "He came to tell me off, you know."

"Why?"

"He couldn't understand why I'd taken Cassie out in the boat."

Jeannie pulled out some cream and smelled it. "It's sour. We're going to have to drink it black."

"No problem."

"It seems to me you had good reason to get Cassie away from those two."

"Actually, Jasmine attacked him first—with a switchblade."

"Good heavens!"

"Jake showed me the injury. It could have killed him. When I walked in, he'd just disarmed her."

Jeannie plunked herself down on a chair. "Blimey."

Maggie shrugged. "I don't know what I can do about it now."

"Not much. So what are your plans?"

"Obviously, no court case." She let her mind roam over the possibilities but felt just too tired to make any decision. "I'd like to just stay put and have some time to recover."

Jeannie got up and poured the coffee. "Good idea."

"I'm sorry about all this. It must have hurt your business."

"Are you kidding? The news coverage put this motel on the map."

Maggie lifted her brows. "Heck of a way to get publicity."

Jeannie laughed. "Next time we'll take out an advertisement. Anyway, I need to get back to work. Are you going to be all right?"

"I'll be fine. Thanks."

Jeannie lifted her cup of coffee. "I'll take this with me."

After Jeannie left, Maggie poured her coffee into the sink. She was jittery enough without adding caffeine. Yes, she needed to face what had happened, but for now, she just needed to get out.

She headed to her car, got in, and rolled down the windows. She sat for a moment and let the scent of the hills calm her. She started the engine and pulled onto Ponderosa Drive, but some cows were blocking the road. They stared at her with their blank faces and ear tags. She waved her hand out the window, but they didn't budge. Finally, she gave a few honks, and they trotted off to a nearby field.

She parked in front of Maynard's and walked across the street to Trudy's Hair Salon.

"I'll take you right away," Trudy said.

"Are you sure?"

Trudy gave her a no-nonsense look. "Of course. I'm not letting you walk around town like that."

Maggie followed her to the sink. Although leaning back hurt her neck, the sensation of shampoo and hot water being massaged into her scalp felt wonderful. Trudy wrapped Maggie's head in a towel and took her over to a station.

She gently took hold of Maggie's uneven hair and met her eyes in the mirror. "Did he do this?"

Tears welled up, and Maggie could only nod.

"I'm going to get you all fixed up."

An hour and a half later, Maggie had a shorter, layered cut with copper highlights. Trudy gave her a pair of dangly earrings from the display case. "Put them on."

She stood in front of the mirror. The earrings sparkled against her neck, and she felt like a weight had been removed. "Thank you."

"You're welcome."

When she sauntered into Maynard's, a number of people turned in their chairs, and it wasn't just because she had a great new hairstyle. Everyone had heard about the car chase and shooting. She'd achieved notoriety.

Lily came over, coffeepot in hand. "Sorry I didn't get to the hospital."

"That's all right."

Maynard stepped out. "Maggie, could you come in here, please?"

Maynard was being polite—not a good sign. She followed him to the kitchen.

Kyle dropped his spatula, ran over, and grabbed her in a bear hug.

"OK, OK, back to work," Maynard said. He didn't look so polite now. In fact, his face had just turned an interesting shade of purple. Was he angry that she hadn't shown up for work? *Jeesh.* It wasn't like she didn't have a good excuse.

"What's wrong?" she asked.

"I just can't figure out how you could be so stupid."

"Pardon?"

"Going out with a guy like that."

"Carlo?"

He placed his hands on his hips. "Who the hell do you think I'm talking about?"

As she examined the floor, feeling about two feet tall, it hit her—Maynard cared. He'd been worried about her. She looked up. "I guess I was pretty stupid."

He glanced at the Tensor bandage. "How you going to work with that?"

She shrugged. "It's just a sprain. Give me a few days, and I'll be fine."

Maynard scrutinized her. "So Jake came to the rescue?"

"Yes."

He frowned. "You steer clear of him."

"Jake?"

"Yeah."

Jeepers, she wouldn't be standing here without Jake. "Why?"

He nodded knowingly. "Wife's back, and wife always trumps girlfriend. She's a real looker, you know."

Now it was Maggie's turn to be ticked. "*What*, and I'm the ugly duckling?"

Maynard chuckled. "You're a looker too . . . in your own way . . . I guess."

"Thanks, I think."

He smiled. "Did you eat?"

"No." She wasn't sure if she was even hungry after this conversation.

"Have some lunch. It's on the house."

She stepped through the swinging doors and sat at a table by the window.

Lily came over. "Maynard giving you a bad time?"

"A little, but he did offer me a meal on the house."

Lily placed a hand on Maggie's shoulder. "Girl, did you destroy the decoy?"

"Yeah. I guess you'll have to come up with a new prank."

"Nah—they're fixing it. What would you like?"

Maggie smiled. "Toast."

"No way. I'm bringing you an omelet." Lily smiled and walked away.

Chapter 28

THE RECEPTIONIST AT THE COUNSELING CENTER LOOKED up as she spoke on the phone. Maggie still had time to turn around and walk out.

A woman, somewhere in her fifties with long black hair streaked with gray, stepped out of an office. "Maggie Jackson?"

Maggie nodded.

"I'm Beatrice Jefferson." She wore silver etched earrings, a brown T-shirt, and gray dress slacks.

Maggie extended her hand. "Pleased to meet you."

"Shall we go in?"

The window offered a view of the river. Framed Indian art decorated the walls, and a basket of dried sage filled the room with the subtle smell of the hills.

Beatrice gestured toward a black couch. "Please have a seat." She glanced inside a manila file folder. "I see you're here under the victim services program."

"Yes."

"I heard about the incident. It was in the local paper."

Maggie shrugged. "Everybody has."

"Sometimes it helps if you just tell me what happened."

"That night?"

"Start at the beginning. When did you meet Carlo? I'm going to let you do all the talking, and I'm going to listen." Beatrice folded her hands in her lap.

"I met Carlo the day he hired me. He owned the Vancouver restaurant, La Fama. We started dating, and pretty soon we were spending most of our time together."

She continued, describing how Carlo asked her to pick up supplies, her discomfort at doing so and her subsequent arrest. She told of Carlo showing up at the motel, the harrowing drive, and his attempt to kill her, which resulted in his own death.

"Then I passed out and woke up in an ambulance on the way to the Lahara hospital." Maggie was breathless but somehow relieved to have spewed it all out.

Beatrice nodded. "When a client tells their narrative, I watch for signs of distress. You seemed quite agitated."

"I am. I barely sleep, and I wake up in a panic. I even thought I saw Carlo walking down the street. I forced myself to go over, and the man looked nothing like him. I feel like I'm losing my mind."

Beatrice met her eyes. "You're not losing your mind. These are all symptoms of post-traumatic stress disorder."

"Really?"

"Yes. Did your doctor give you any medication?"

"Benzodiazepine. She told me to use it as needed. I don't get it. Why now? When I was in the car with Carlo, I wasn't panicking—I was planning my escape."

Beatrice nodded. "When a person goes into battle, the stress hormones are there to keep them alive. When the danger is over, these hormones don't just stop." She took a pamphlet off a table and gave it to Maggie. "These are some breathing and relaxation exercises. They'll help." She glanced at her watch. "I'm sorry, but our time is up. Would you like to book another session?"

"Sure."

"Same time next Tuesday?"

"Yes, that works for me."

Beatrice smiled. "I know that there's lots we didn't get to. Be patient."

"It helped. Thank you."

Outside, Maggie felt like a burden had been lifted. She wasn't going crazy. She just needed time to heal. If her sprained ankle could heal, so could the rest of her. She was in no hurry to return to Vancouver—not when she felt this bad. She might still be paying rent on her apartment, but some things were more important than money, first and foremost her mental and physical health.

Jake played a board game with Cassie, while Eva, the social worker, sat in the corner reading over her notes. He rolled the dice and moved the marker two places.

"Daddy, I want to go home," Cassie said.

"Soon, I hope."

Cassie clutched the dice. "How soon?"

Eva looked up.

"I'm not sure. Hey, I'm kind of bored with this game. How about we go outside?"

"OK."

He reached for Cassie, threw her over his shoulder and carried her, giggling, outside. It had started to rain, but there were worse things than a child getting a wet.

Unfortunately, Eva followed them out. Ten minutes later as he pushed Cassie on the tire swing, Eva approached, an umbrella over her head. "Sorry, but it's four o'clock."

Right on cue, Sandra came out. "Come on, Cassie. We're going to watch a movie. The other kids are waiting for you."

Jake gave Cassie a hug and nodded his thanks to Sandra.

He'd taken to parking down the street where he wouldn't have to look back. He was almost at the truck when Jasmine drove up in her white MG convertible.

She pulled over to the side of the road and rolled down the window. "Hey, Jake."

"How'd you get your car?"

"Mike helped me. We met at the bar last night. This morning, he drove me to the Lahara airport to turn in the rental car. Then we went to the house to jump-start this."

She was baiting him, and he wasn't biting. "You had no right. I wasn't there."

She smiled. "Remember, it's my house, too. Besides, I had to go in and get my things."

Crap. He should have changed the locks. He'd do it tomorrow, even if the house was still technically half hers. "Great. Glad to get that stuff out of there."

"How come you moved my clothes out of the bedroom? I had to go all over the house looking for them."

This conversation was over. He got into the truck and revved the engine to drown her out. She waved before speeding off.

He drove straight to the river rafting launch and unlocked the supply shed. Life jackets were hung up in a disorderly fashion. He picked up a Styrofoam container covered in hardened ketchup and threw it in the trash.

When the van arrived, the tourists got out, talking and laughing despite the rain. Jake walked over to a man with a shaved head and a big smile. "How was it?"

"Fantastic."

"Where are you from?"

"Port Moody. Definitely want to try that overnight rafting trip sometime."

Jake smiled. "Book early. That one really fills up."

The man got into his car. Jake waved and walked down to the water. Glenn and Mike had unloaded the boats and tied them to the dock, ready for the next trip.

"A word, Mike," Jake said.

"Something wrong, boss?" Glenn asked.

"It's between Mike and me."

Glenn walked away, and Mike turned to him. "Hey, Jake."

"You took Jasmine to the house to get her car."

Mike met his eyes. "Yeah, was there a problem with that?"

"I don't want her anywhere near the house."

Mike gave him a questioning look. "She said you'd asked me to help her out—that you were too busy."

Crap. Mike was telling the truth. When was he ever going to learn that Jasmine lied about everything? "I never asked that. She lied. Don't worry about it. A word of advice, though."

"Yeah?" The poor guy looked like he'd been sideswiped.

"Next time she asks you to do something, run like hell."

Chapter 29

MAGGIE LET HERSELF IN THE BACK DOOR OF THE restaurant to find Kyle warming up the grills. The floors smelled of bleach, and everything looked spotless. "Hey, Kyle. The kitchen looks great."

"Thanks."

She pulled her waitress uniform off the hook. "When's Maynard coming in?"

"Around noon."

She unlocked the front door and turned the sign to *Open*. Customers sauntered in and placed their hats on the tables. Just to humor her, Kyle placed various garnishes on each plate: a sprig of parsley, a radish cut open to look like a flower, a cherry tomato. Customers eyed these tidbits suspiciously. Some nibbled at them, others moved them to the side of their plates.

Most of the breakfast crowd had left when Jake and Marie walked in.

When Marie went to the restroom, Maggie hurried over. "Jake, I've been subpoenaed to the hearing tomorrow."

He creased his brow. "Why?"

"I don't know. I already made my police report. What could they possibly want to know that I haven't already told them?"

He shook his head. "Don't know."

She tipped her head. "How's Marie holding up?"

"Not very well. Jasmine still won't talk to her. We visited Cassie yesterday, and Cassie asked Marie to take her home to Vancouver, but even that's not allowed." He ran a hand through his hair. "The sooner this is settled the better." He signaled that Marie had come out of the restroom.

Maggie busied herself with other customers. It was so absurd—Marie sitting there with her son-in-law while her daughter was staying a block away at the Rosetown hotel. No sooner had Jasmine entered her mind than there she was, walking by as if she didn't have a care in the world.

Marie raced out the door and grasped her daughter's hand. She said something that couldn't be heard through the glass, and Jasmine responded angrily. Marie tried to hug her, but Jasmine turned and walked away.

Marie doubled over, like she was about to collapse. Jake ran out, put his arm around her, and led her inside. A lump formed in Maggie's throat. Marie was seriously ill. Surely Jasmine could at least be civil. And why was Jasmine fighting to get Cassie back now? If she'd been concerned for her daughter, she would have made at least one phone call in the last year. Her silence had been deafening. Surely no judge would ignore it.

"Just take me home," Marie cried. "Please."

People tried not to stare as Jake led her out. Maggie let out the breath she'd been holding in and forced herself to get back to work.

That evening, Jake got Marie settled on the couch with a cup of tea.

Marie looked up at him. "Isn't it strange? I never came to visit when you and Jasmine were together."

Jake nodded. He couldn't tell her that he'd suggested it, but Jasmine had said no.

Marie took a sip of tea. "Can you join me?"

"Sure." He poured himself some tea.

"I asked her to come home," Marie began. "I said she didn't have to be with him—that we'd get her help. She asked what gave me the right to screw with her head. What could she mean by that?"

Jake sighed. "She doesn't believe the abuse happened."

"I've thought of that. I've read about it. I'm just having trouble believing it." Marie paused as if thinking things through. "I have to stand up to her. I'm going to tell the court everything that happened, and why she is the way she is. All I want to know is that when I die, Cassie will never meet that man."

Jake put his cup on the coffee table. "You're not going to die."

She smiled. "Jake, we all die someday."

He leaned forward. "I meant not right away. The doctor said you had a good chance."

"I think I'll have a whole lot better chance if I do the right thing. I couldn't stand seeing Cassie upset like she was yesterday."

"Neither could I. She has no idea why she can't just come home."

A determined look crossed Marie's fact. "Then let's make it happen. If my daughter never speaks to me again, so be it."

Chapter

30

THE COURT CLERK SWORE HER IN, AND MAGGIE TOOK THE stand as a stern-looking Judge Donaldson looked on. Jake and Marie sat beside their lawyer, Mr. Nathan Walker, a middle-aged man wearing an expensive-looking suit. On the other side of the courtroom, Jasmine sat by her lawyer, Ms. Miranda Wong, a smart-looking woman who looked to be in her thirties. Chief Constable Frank MacKenzie and Anne Metcalfe, the social worker, sat side by side, and Mark was there as well. Other than the two guards at the door and a stenographer, they were the only people at the hearing.

Maggie's heart beat wildly as Jake's lawyer, Mr. Walker, approached. He gave her a quick, businesslike smile. "Would you please tell the court what happened on July twenty-second?"

"I was babysitting for Jake when Jasmine came home after being missing for ten months."

"Ms. Jackson, would you please point out Cassie's mother?"

Maggie pointed at Jasmine, and Jasmine gave her a warm smile. *Oh, God.* She felt disconcerted.

"Thank you. Please go on."

She glanced at Jake, and he gave a slight nod. She remembered his warning that Carlo might smile to get her to let her guard down. She fixed her eyes on Nathan Walker and described Jake arriving home, the ensuing argument between Jake and Jasmine, and how she'd seen Jake holding Jasmine face down on the floor, her arm twisted up behind her back. When she came to the part when Cassie had been taken away in a police cruiser, she stopped.

"Thank you," Mr. Walker said. He turned to the judge. "No further questions, Your Honor."

Jasmine's lawyer, Ms. Miranda Wong, approached. "Was Jake paying you to babysit?"

"No."

"Why was that?"

"We were friends."

"Close enough friends that you'd look after Cassie for three days without pay?"

Mr. Walker stood up. "Objection. Leading the witness."

"Sustained."

Miranda Wong picked up a file folder. "The incident you described took place on July twenty-second, but you didn't make a police report until July twenty-sixth. Is this correct?"

"Yes."

"Jake made his police report on July twenty-third. Did you ask him about it?"

"No."

"You said you were friends."

"Yes, but I wasn't speaking to him at that time. In fact, I didn't speak to him for a week after the incident."

Miranda Wong pulled a paper out of the file folder and handed it to Maggie. "Read this please—not out loud, just to yourself."

It was her own report. She read it through then looked up.

Ms. Wong smiled. "Would you like to change or retract anything?"

"No."

Miranda Wong tilted her head. "You are one-hundred-percent sure that all the details are correct?"

Doubt. Then suddenly, Maggie no longer saw Miranda Wong—she saw Carlo. How she'd see things he was doing, and he'd then plant a seed of doubt until she no longer knew if she could trust her own eyes. She squared her shoulders. "Yes, one hundred percent. All the details are accurate."

Miranda Wong took the report from her hands and turned to the judge. "No further questions, Your Honor."

Maggie left the courtroom. She'd told the truth, and whatever came of it was out of her hands.

Three hours later, she was sitting in the motel courtyard, sipping a glass of wine and worrying about what was going to happen to Cassie, when Jake pulled up. He got out and walked over. His posture was relaxed and he had a broad smile. She put down her glass and ran toward him.

He picked her up and spun her around. "I pick up Cassie tomorrow. The judge granted me full custody."

She felt flooded with relief. "That's great!"

She pulled over a second lawn chair. "So Jasmine can't see Cassie at all?"

"Supervised visits only. With a knife attack and the abandonment issue, she was deemed unfit and lost custody."

He met her eyes. "Your testimony helped."

"How?"

"Because it showed my report was true and that Jasmine was a liar." Jake pushed a hand through his hair. "The day after the incident, Jasmine and I both made police reports, neither of us aware that you'd come in and seen us during the argument. She said that I attacked her, and that she stabbed me in self-defense then ran out the door. I said she attacked me and I disarmed her and held her down on the floor."

"And my report lined up with yours."

"Yes, and Miranda Wong hoped to discredit it in some way."

"By implying that you may have influenced what I wrote?"

Jake nodded. "But we weren't talking. So that was a good thing. And when my lawyer asked you to describe the incident, you repeated what you'd written almost verbatim. It would be hard to describe all those details if you'd just written what I told you to say."

Maggie picked up her glass of wine. "Ms. Wong tried to make me doubt myself."

Jake smiled. "She tried, but you didn't."

She closed her eyes. Cassie was safe—never to be turned over to an abuser. All the stress of the day dissipated, and she opened her eyes to see Jake observing her.

He reached for her hand. "Let's go out and celebrate."

She tilted her head. "Chinese food?"

His dimple appeared. "No."

"Should I dress up?"

He glanced at her. "No, what you're wearing is fine, but you might want to bring a jacket."

Chapter
31

THE RIVER ALMOST PURRED ITS CONTENTMENT AS THEY motored downstream. Maggie looked fantastic with her new hairstyle and a pair of sparkling earrings dangling against her neck. Jake pulled the boat up onto a small, sandy beach.

He laid out the blanket and pulled out the picnic basket. A bottle of wine, bread, some corned beef and mustard—since he knew that was a hit—a block of cheese, and grapes. He'd even brought along a candle, though if a wind came up, it wouldn't be much good.

Maggie leaned back on her hands. "What a lovely spot."

"There are places like this all along the river." He tried unsuccessfully to light the candle. *Definitely not going to work.* He poured them each a glass of red wine then held up his glass. "To you being safe, and to Cassie coming home."

She raised her glass and took a sip. "You didn't tell me about Marie's role in the hearing."

"It was hard for her. She explained that her health and her age didn't allow her to take Cassie for the long term and asked that

I be given full custody. She was honest about Jasmine's mental health and the danger that Tom Schmidt posed."

"It must have been difficult to say all that with Jasmine present."

"It was, but she did it for Cassie's sake. She's back at my place having a rest. It was draining, but she's so relieved that Cassie's future is secure." He sliced off a piece of cheese and handed it to her. "So what about you? What are your plans?"

"My mother wants me to move to Calgary. I prefer Vancouver, but for now I'm just going to stay put, recover, and try to figure myself out. I'm still having panic attacks and a lot of trouble sleeping."

"Anybody would feel that way after going through what you did."

"What about you? Jasmine stabbed you, and Carlo almost killed you."

He leaned back. How could he tell her that the only panic he felt was at the thought of her leaving? "I'm OK. I live on the edge with my job, so I'm used to life-and-death situations."

When they finished eating, she helped him put the dishes back into the picnic basket. He poured her another glass of wine and turned his body around so they could both watch the sunset. Swallows swooped down in pursuit of mosquitoes, and every once in a while, a salmon jumped. He put a hand on her thigh. "How's your ankle?"

"Recovering."

All the bruising had left her face, but she had little dark circles under her eyes. He hated to think of her lying awake. He put a hand under one of her sparkly earrings and kissed her. She tasted like red wine. Her eyes remained closed, so he kissed her again.

He lay back, and she placed her head on his chest. He felt like spending the night here, just holding her and staring up at the stars, but it was getting chilly. "I guess we'd better go."

She shivered and nodded.

When they parked at the motel, he leaned over and kissed her again. This was his last night before he became a full-fledged single father, with all the responsibilities that entailed. Almost as if she'd heard the thought, she asked, "Would you like to come in?"

As she unlocked the door, his heart went into overtime. Inside, she motioned for him to take a seat, then sat on his knee, took his face in both hands, and kissed him again. As the kisses intensified, he reached for the top button of her blouse and didn't stop until each button was undone. She had beautiful breasts under a white lacy bra. For a good minute, he just took her in with his eyes before reaching up for the clasp. She grasped his hands. "Shouldn't you call Marie?"

"Why?"

"To tell her you won't be home tonight."

God, he loved this woman with her wide smile and big, luminous eyes.

She kissed him again as he brought out his phone.

Chapter
32

CASSIE SEARCHED THROUGH THE UNMADE BED AT SANDRA'S house for her pink dog stuffy. "I found it."

Jake turned to Sandra, who stood in her housecoat. "Thank you."

"You're welcome." Sandra gave Cassie a hug.

Outside, the air had that hint of crispness that said summer was coming to an end. Jake had his daughter by the hand, he'd just had the most amazing night of his life, and his truck looked as good as new. Life didn't get much better than this.

When they arrived home, Susie ran in circles then licked Cassie's face.

"Let's unpack those bags." Jake said.

As Cassie stuffed her clothes into the drawers, he looked at the dark green bedspread and beige walls with new eyes. "You and I are going to paint this room. What color do you like?"

"Pink!"

"Then pink it is. Come on. I'll make you breakfast."

Maggie put on a short jean skirt and a white peasant blouse. She applied makeup and put on her new earrings. She was just tidying up the living room when Jake and Cassie knocked on the open door.

She hugged Cassie.

Cassie pointed to the Tensor bandage. "What's that?"

"I had an accident. But I'm fine. Hey, I missed you while you were staying at Sandra's." Cassie smiled. Maggie picked up her purse. "Where are we going?"

"I can't tell you a thing," Cassie said.

Jake put a hand on Cassie's shoulder. "She means it's a surprise. Do you mind if we stop briefly at Connie's? She's got a circuit breaker that keeps blowing, and she's asked me to take a look at it."

"No problem."

As they walked to the truck, Cassie slipped her hand into Maggie's.

"I'll bet Susie was glad to see you," Maggie said.

Cassie smiled. "Uh-huh."

Maggie pointed to a hawk. "Look!"

Cassie looked up. "Why's it doing that?"

"What?"

"Going round and round."

"It's hunting for a mouse or rodent."

"What's a rodent?"

"It's a little mammal, like a mouse or rat."

"What's a mammal?"

Jake glanced over and gave Maggie a wink.

"A mammal is an animal that gives birth to live babies. You know instead of laying eggs like birds do."

"Oh."

Jake opened the truck's passenger door, and they climbed in.

As they drove down the hill toward town, Cassie made her pink dog stuffy hop up and down. "Doggy is a mammal."

Maggie put an arm around Cassie and gave her a squeeze. "Dogs are mammals." She touched Cassie's nose. "And so are you."

Cassie giggled.

When they arrived at Connie's house, Jake jumped out. "I'll just be a minute. You two wait here."

Connie opened the door, and Jake signaled that Maggie and Cassie should come after all.

"I'm so relieved to see you in one piece." Connie looked at the Tensor bandage. "Well, almost in one piece."

"Cassie, this is Mrs. Day."

Connie smiled. "Hi, Cassie. Would you like to come in for a minute? There's something I want to show you."

They stepped inside.

"Surprise!" rang out.

The house was full of people.

Connie hugged Maggie. "I wanted to have a party to celebrate your safe return. It just took me a couple of weeks to get it organized."

Maggie placed her hand over her heart and found her voice. "Thank you."

Jake took Cassie out to the backyard, and Maggie began to make the rounds. When she reached the kitchen, where Ed was preparing a salmon, she kissed his cheek. He blushed, and she pointed at his black apron: *Kiss the Cook*.

Outside, Cassie and a small group of children were running around. Jake threw an arm around Maggie's shoulders. "Surprised?"

"I was. Cassie knew about this?"

He smiled. "She did, and I thought she was going to spill the beans."

Maggie couldn't believe that they'd pulled it off. "But I saw a picnic basket in the back of the truck."

"I figured you'd see that."

She poked his side. "Sneaky."

He kissed the side of her head. "There's a pasta salad in the truck. I'll get it."

Gabriela walked over with two teenagers. "This is my daughter, Carmela, and my son, Alfonso." Both of them had black hair and big brown eyes like their mother.

A tall, thin man with a slightly crooked nose joined them. "I'm Father Norman."

"Our priest," Gabriela said.

"And Mark's friend," he added.

Mark called for everyone's attention and said the blessing. The tables were laden with salmon, barbecued chicken, salads, and buns, and Maggie was suddenly famished. She loaded her plate until it couldn't hold another item and sat beside Jake and Cassie to eat.

"I see you've gotten your appetite back," Jack said.

She laughed. "Nothing like good food and good friends to do that for a person."

"What about last night?"

Her cheeks grew warm. "That too."

When everyone had eaten, Gabriela turned on the sound system, and people got up to dance. Jake took Cassie and twirled her out to the grassy dance floor.

Maggie sipped a coffee, and Father Norman sat down beside her, his eyes on Gabriela and Mark, who had joined in the dancing.

"A little romance there?" he asked.

"Maybe. You don't mind that he's not Catholic?"

He chuckled. "I may convert him yet."

The slow strains of a country waltz began. Jake extended his hand, and Maggie limped out. He took her carefully in his arms. He'd already learned where all the still-tender spots were. He smelled good—like soap and river water. She looked up.

He smiled. "You know I love you."

"You told me that last night."

"Just wanted to be sure you knew."

"Love you too."

He kissed her, and just the brush of his lips sent a shiver of anticipation through her body. The previous night had been emotional, earth-shattering. And Jake had been so thoughtful.

The music turned to rock 'n' roll, and Cassie appeared by their side. Maggie pointed to her bandaged leg and excused herself so that father and daughter could have a dance.

Connie strolled over. "Having a good time?"

The dishes had all been cleared away, and a few men were taking down the folding tables. "Yes. This was a lot of work for you."

"I had many helpers." A concerned look crossed Connie's face. "How are you feeling?"

"I'm still a little shaken, but I'll get over it."

Connie shook her head. "I'm sorry you went through all that."

"Me too." A part of her still couldn't believe that Carlo was dead and her life was her own again.

Jake and Cassie returned from their dance. Connie tipped her head. "Would you three like to come over for lunch sometime?"

"We'd love to," Maggie said as Jake and Cassie both nodded in agreement.

The sky had turned dark and the air was chilly when they finally made their way to the truck. Cassie fell asleep before they reached the motel.

Jake looked across his sleeping daughter. "I'll walk you to the door."

"No. Don't wake her."

His eyes became hopeful. "Want to come over?"

She shook her head. "I'm working tomorrow, and I'm exhausted." She leaned across and gave him a kiss. Cassie stirred.

He smiled. "I'll call you."

Chapter 33

MAGGIE CLASPED HER HANDS IN FRONT OF HER. COMING TO these counseling sessions was like drudging up sludge from the bottom of a lake.

Beatrice met her eyes. "Why didn't you just go to the police with your suspicions?"

"I felt sorry for Carlo. His whole family was murdered when he was a teenager. I didn't want to be the one responsible for putting him in jail."

"Seems like he was the one responsible for putting himself in jail, not you."

"I know."

Beatrice leaned back in her chair, her eyes soft and understanding. "Did you think about leaving?"

"All the time, but I didn't." A window was open, and Maggie wished she could fly out and disappear from this place of pain inside herself.

"Why not?" Beatrice asked.

That was the million-dollar question. She tried to remember what it had been like. "I loved him."

"Yes."

"And I didn't have many other friends in Vancouver."

Beatrice nodded.

"And I didn't want to hurt him. He suffered from depression. Sometimes he talked about suicide. I mean, what if I left, and he killed himself?" *Bingo.*

Beatrice gave her a moment before speaking. "Did you ever think that he talked about suicide to control you?"

"Not at the time."

"How about now?"

Maggie let out the breath she'd been holding in. "Well, I left, and he never killed himself." She glanced up at the corner of the room before meeting Beatrice's eyes. "He tried to kill me instead. So yeah, I think he did a lot of things to play me. He even used to get me to straighten my hair."

Beatrice tipped her head. "Tell me more."

"He'd say I looked a mess and tell me to do something about it. I'd refuse. Then he'd ignore me for hours, even days. Then finally he'd say, 'What's the big deal?' And I'd ask myself the same question—what was the big deal? It was only a little thing."

"Then you'd do as he asked?"

"Yes." Maggie felt stabs of embarrassment. It wasn't a little thing, and how had she lost so much confidence that she'd let a man control like that?

Beatrice folded her hands in her lap. "How did Carlo behave when you gave in?"

Maggie closed her eyes and pictured Carlo's face. "He was happy. I was happy. At least I thought I was happy. Actually, I was pretty resentful."

Beatrice leaned forward. "Maggie, you were in an abusive relationship. Carlo knew that if he made your life miserable enough, he could get you to do whatever he wanted just to make the discomfort stop. It's called negative reinforcement. Look it up online. It's far more powerful than positive reinforcement."

Maggie felt a jolt. Her? In an abusive relationship? *Shit.* "How did this happen to me?"

"It happens to a lot of us."

"You?"

Beatrice nodded, her face open and vulnerable. "A long time ago. Before I knew what I know now."

"So how do I keep it from happening again?"

"Knowledge. Observation. Listen to that inner pilot—it's there for a reason. If something doesn't feel right, it probably isn't."

Maggie glanced at her watch. "My time's up."

Beatrice smiled. "I'll see you next week."

A chicken baked in the oven. Jake planned to cook rice instead of potatoes. He had to show her that he was more than just a meat-and-potatoes guy.

Maggie rapped on the door.

He hugged her. "How was your day?"

"Good. My parents arrive tomorrow."

She was wearing a blouse, white jeans, and a pair of sandals. He glanced down at her toenails painted a sexy bright orange and found himself imagining her feet intertwined with his own. "Already?" he asked.

She smiled and tilted her head. "You could help me entertain them."

Whoa. He thought of their interrogation methods. He needed to pick a low-key activity. "Do they like fishing?"

"Dad does."

"I know of a great little lake about an hour from here. I keep a rowboat there."

"I'll ask them." Cassie skipped into the kitchen. "So what did you do today?" Maggie asked.

"I went to Sandra's. Daddy painted my room."

"What color is it?"

"Pink. Come see!" Cassie took her hand, and they walked down the hall.

Jake washed some green beans. Dating as a single father was turning out to have its challenges. It was hard to find time to be alone with Maggie. She acted like she didn't mind, but tonight, once Cassie was asleep, he was going to show her that it wasn't all about kids for him. He could be just as exciting as the next guy.

The walls were pale pink. The dresser and end tables had been painted white.

"I love this," Maggie said.

Cassie climbed up on the bed. Susie jumped up behind her.

"Is Susie allowed on the bed?"

"No." Cassie started to jump.

Maggie took Cassie's hands. "Stop jumping and tell Susie to get down."

Cassie put her arm around the dog. "Get down."

Susie licked Cassie's face.

Maggie shook her head. Better to demonstrate. She took the dog by the collar. "Down, girl." It looked like Jake had done more than just paint. "Is that a *Moana* bedspread?"

"Yeah. Daddy and I went shopping."

Maggie took an elephant stuffy and made it jump and talk. "I love it. I love it. I looooove it!"

Cassie giggled.

Maggie smiled. "Want your hair done?"

Cassie nodded.

She'd just finished Cassie's braids when Jake poked his head through the door. "Supper is ready."

They ate on the deck. The river ran low, and a warm breeze drifted off the hills. Now that she was feeling better, she needed to apply for some chef jobs, but it was going to be hard to leave this place. She glanced at Jake's blue eyes. It was going to be hard to leave him. They'd been using the L word—often. He hadn't asked her to stay, and she hadn't said she would leave for sure, but they both knew she had an apartment and another life waiting for her in Vancouver.

After supper, they walked down to the beach. Cassie threw sticks for Susie. Jake wore a dress shirt, jeans, and a cowboy hat that she'd never seen on him before. They swung Cassie up between them as they walked back to the house.

Maggie went out to the deck to admire the view, while Jake tucked Cassie into bed. Did she really have to go back to Vancouver? Wouldn't there be chef jobs in Lahara? She was still contemplating her options when Jake wrapped his arms around her. She leaned back against him. The wind caught his cowboy hat and blew it off his head.

She raced to pick it up. "Is Cassie asleep?"

"Yes."

She put the hat on his head and stood on tiptoe to kiss him. She took a step closer, ran her hands down his back, and felt him respond. She stopped and searched his eyes. He squeezed her hand and led her inside.

This was it. Rice and chicken, not steak and potatoes. He put Marvin Gaye on the stereo and turned around.

She raised her brows. "I love the hat."

"How would you feel about only the hat?"

She tipped her head. "What do you have in mind?"

He undid the buttons of his shirt. She giggled. Encouraged, he pulled off the shirt. He reached for the rose on the coffee table and put it in his mouth, but quickly let it fall. He'd missed one thorn when he'd prepared this charade.

She clutched her belly and laughed.

Cassie came out of the bedroom. "Daddy, why is your shirt off?"

He grabbed his shirt, his face burning. "I was hot."

Maggie smiled. "He was *really, really* hot."

Cassie rubbed her eyes. "I can't sleep."

Maggie opened her arms, and Cassie joined her on the couch.

"Why are you laughing?" Cassie said.

"Because your dad is so funny."

Jake put on his shirt, turned off the music, and put the rose back in the vase. He sat beside them, reached for a children's book, and began to read. When Cassie started to nod off, he picked her up and carried her back to bed, battling frustration. Why would a hot single woman like Maggie be interested in someone like him? He'd made a fool of himself. He walked back out, too embarrassed to meet her eyes.

"Jake," she said.

He looked up. Her jeans were off, her blouse was unbuttoned, and she was wearing the cowboy hat. He raced over and took her hands.

"Do you have a lock on your bedroom door?"

"Yes."

She smiled. "How about we move in there?"

Maggie woke up with the moonlight shining in. Susie was barking. What time was it? Jake was sound asleep. She lay on her tummy and ran her hand over his muscular shoulder, pulling herself up to kiss his lips. But Susie just wouldn't let up. She got up and opened the kitchen door.

Taillights!

She raced back and shook Jake. He opened his eyes and pulled her toward him.

"Somebody's out there!"

He leapt from the bed and ran to the door. "I don't see anything."

"I saw taillights. Do you think it was Jasmine?"

"I know it was her. It's not the first time."

"What's wrong with her?" Maggie's heart was racing. If Jasmine could stab Jake, what else could she do? Sneak in and kill them while they slept?

"She's crazy. I wish she'd get help, I really do." He met Maggie's eyes. "Don't worry. I've changed all the locks." He sighed. "Sorry. All I can do is ignore her until she grows tired of these games."

"Could Marie talk to her?"

He shook his head. "Jasmine still refuses to have anything to do with her mother."

The clock read 3:00 a.m. "What does she want, coming around at a time like this?"

"Like I said, she's crazy. At least she's gone. Let's go back to bed." He kissed her.

They climbed into bed, and Maggie snuggled into his arms. "What's Cassie going to say when I'm here in the morning?"

"Probably ask you to make pancakes."

She lifted her head. "I can't sleep."

He kissed her slowly. "I guess we'll just have to find some way to kill the time."

Chapter 34

MAGGIE DROVE, AND JAKE POINTED OUT LANDMARKS. HER parents and Cassie shared the back seat. Susie lay in the rear of the station wagon where hopefully, she was not figuring out how to open the picnic basket. The rolling fields stretched out for miles around them, and every once in a while a dilapidated log cabin would appear, causing her father to yell, "Stop! I want a picture." At this rate, it was going to take a lot longer than an hour to get to the lake.

After turning off the highway onto a gravel road, they drove through a forested area and arrived at a small lake with a sandy beach, a dock, and a few rowboats tied up. No one was in sight.

Jake and Ray pulled out the fishing rods and tackle box.

Jake put a hand on Cassie's shoulder. "Want to go fishing?"

She nodded.

He took out some sunscreen, rubbed it on Cassie and himself, and handed it to Ray.

After they left, Maggie and her mother went to the outhouse and changed into bathing suits. They laid out their blankets where they could lean their backs against a log. Susie whined at the water's edge.

"Susie, come here," Maggie called.

The dog returned and found a shady area to lie down. Maggie leaned back, enjoying the warmth of the sun's rays. "This is the life, isn't it?"

Karen set down her paperback novel. "You've changed."

"I have?"

"Yes. There was a time when you would have been bored to death with a place like this."

Maggie took a moment before answering. "I guess there was."

Karen put on a broad-brimmed hat and slathered sunscreen on her arms. She had the same red hair and pale skin as Maggie. "When you go back to the city, you'll be a different person."

"*If* I go back to the city."

"You're thinking of staying here?"

"Why not?"

"What about your career?"

Maggie sat straight up. "Mom, I'm a chef. I can cook anywhere."

"I always felt that you could do more."

Maggie fought for composure to mask the hurt. She was never going to be good enough for her mother. "So could you!"

"What are you talking about?"

"Your bookshelf is lined with medical books. Why not take some courses?"

A look crossed her mother's face. Sadness, pain, regret—Maggie couldn't quite put her finger on it, and for one of the first times in her life, she felt sympathy toward her. "Mom, it's never too late."

Karen's eyes filled with tears. "I've been too hard on you."

Maggie, determined to not back down, mustered up her courage. "Yes, you have. Now ask me what my dream is."

"To be a chef. You already told me that."

"Mom, ask me."

Karen pulled out a tissue, dried her tears, and blew her nose. "What is your dream?"

"To own a very successful restaurant."

"Really?" Her face lit up. It was like she'd finally heard her. "Could Dad and I help? Financially, I mean?"

"Thanks for the offer, but I'd like to do it on my own." The last thing she needed was to let her parents help out. Her mother would show up wanting to work there.

Karen smiled. "You and Rob were the best thing to ever happen to me."

"What about Dad?"

She looked out to the middle of the lake. "Dad too. I've had a good life. My job wasn't exactly what I wanted, but it wasn't so bad. Maybe I'm just ready to retire and try something new. I can't see myself starting a second career, but I might be interested in volunteering at the Red Cross." She took a sip of her water bottle. "It's just that I've been responsible for so long. I don't know how to let up."

"Because of your parent's drinking?"

She nodded. "And I'm a bit of a control freak."

Maggie laughed. "I never thought I'd hear you say it."

Karen shook her head. "I don't see you denying it."

"Nope, so take control now and retire. Your house is paid for. You'd qualify for a pension."

"I'll think about it."

"Good. And sign up for a course. It doesn't have to lead to anything, but it might."

"Gosh, you're getting as bossy as your brother."

"I'll take that as a compliment." Maggie lay on her back and pulled her baseball cap over her face.

She woke up to Cassie's voice. "Maggie, come and see the fish!"

She shook the cobwebs from her brain, put on her flip-flops, and headed down to the dock. Jake opened the cooler to display a medium-sized trout.

She took Cassie's hands and helped her out of the boat. "Are you going to cook that tonight?"

Cassie shrugged and looked at Jake.

"We are," he said.

"Is everybody ready for lunch?"

Ray climbed out. He looked like a tourist in a flowered Hawaiian shirt, baggie shorts, and a Tilley hat. "I'm famished."

As she retrieved the picnic basket from the car, Jake came up behind her, put his hands on her waist and kissed her neck.

Maggie turned and slapped his hand. "Hey, my parents are over there."

He laughed.

After lunch, Karen and Ray asked Jake if they could go for a row.

"Sure," Jake said.

"Would you mind if Cassie came?" Ray asked.

He glanced at Cassie. "Want to go?"

She nodded and took Karen's hand. A look of softness touched her mother's face.

Jake came and stretched out beside Maggie. "How do you like this spot?"

She looked around—green lake, blue sky, deserted beach. "It's lovely."

"I got the feeling that you and your mom were a little tense on the way here."

"True. I was wondering how long before she started in on me. But we had a good talk. I think I might have finally gotten through to her."

"I like your mom. She's got spunk, like you."

"Thanks." Her whole body felt hot. "Want to go for a swim?"

They raced into the water. Not too warm and not too cool, just refreshing. She emerged and pushed the hair off her face. No crowds, no concession stands. Just a dock, an outhouse, and a beach. Jake swam up and kissed her. She wrapped her arms around his neck and kissed him back. His hands were exploring her body in a way that would have her undone in a few minutes if he didn't stop, so she swam away then turned around and splashed him.

He swam over, caught her, and kissed her again. "Stay over tonight."

She bit her lip, wishing with all her heart that she could. "I can't. My parents will want to spend time with me."

He took her hand. "Tomorrow?"

"Maybe."

They jogged out of the water and sat on the blanket, their backs propped against the log.

Jake became serious. "I'm going to get a divorce." He stared at the lake, his jaw taking on a firmness. "Jasmine coming by the house in the middle of the night was too much. I have to establish some boundaries."

Maggie frowned. "Do you think she'll go back to her father?"

"I hope not."

Her parents pulled up to the dock. She could just make out the words *daycare* and *school*. Cassie had become their next interrogation victim, and fortunately, she seemed to like the attention. "I told my mother to quit her job and go back to school."

Jake reached for her hand. "Do you think she will?"

As Karen helped Cassie out of the boat, she looked almost carefree. "You know, I think she just might."

Chapter 35

CASSIE CROUCHED DOWN IN THE MEADOW. "LOOK."

A beetle crawled over a pile of cow dung. Cassie noticed the little things: the contrasting colors of a bumblebee, a magpie's long tail feathers, the unique smell of juniper bush berries.

"What do you think that beetle's doing?" Maggie asked.

Cassie watched it for a minute. "This beetle eats poo."

"I guess it does. Maybe you're going to be a biologist someday."

Cassie stood up. "What's a biologist?"

"A person who studies animals." Cassie looked pleased. "Come on. We've got to get going if we're going to see your dad." They continued their walk. When they reached the river, Maggie took Cassie's hand. "I first saw your dad right here."

"Did he catch a tourist?"

Maggie smiled. "Yes, he was pulling her out of the water."

Cassie knit her brow.

"You know what tourists are, right? The people on the raft."

A look of comprehension crossed Cassie's face. "Oh, I thought they were fish, because Daddy said he catches them."

Maggie laughed. "No, tourists are people who go on a holiday."

They heard shouts, and the raft appeared. Jake followed in the chase boat, white water spraying all around him. He lifted a hand and threw them a kiss as the Zodiac bounced over the waves. He looked like the happiest man on earth.

"Someday, you'll go river rafting," Maggie said.

"You mean on the boat?"

"No, your dad already takes you on his boat. I mean, he'll let you go on the raft." Maggie pointed. "The boat that's out in front."

"Will you come?"

"Sure."

They hiked back to the motel, the afternoon sun on their backs. When they reached the motel, Cassie joined a group of children who were kicking a soccer ball around. Maggie stepped inside, lifted the lid to the spaghetti sauce, and took a taste. She pulled out the ingredients to make a salad then glanced out. The children had disappeared. She found them standing on the fence railing watching the pig, but Cassie was nowhere in sight.

"Where's the little girl with the braids?" Maggie asked.

"Oh, she left," a brown-haired boy said. "Her mom picked her up."

Maggie's heart skipped a beat. "A blonde woman?"

"Yeah, their dog was hurt. They had to take it to the vet."

"Did you see the car?"

"It was blue." The other children nodded.

Maggie sprinted back and called 911.

It had been a great trip, and especially great seeing Maggie and Cassie together. Jake turned the bend, and Maggie was there on the beach, frantically waving her hands over her head. Cassie wasn't with her. A bad feeling hit him, and he gunned the engine.

"What's up?" he yelled.

"Jasmine took Cassie!"

He hauled his boat up onto the beach. "Take over!" he shouted to Glenn.

They raced to the car. Maggie spoke as she drove. "Cassie was playing with a group of children, and they went around to see the pig. Jasmine was waiting there. She told Cassie that Susie was hurt, and they had to take her to the vet. It wasn't Jasmine's car."

Jake ran a hand through his hair. *Crap.* Jasmine had been served with divorce papers that morning. Was this her way of getting even?

At the RCMP detachment, Frank MacKenzie stood with his shoulders squared and his brow knit. "No cars have been rented in her name."

"Try Tom Schmidt," Jake suggested.

Frank nodded and disappeared into the back.

Five minutes later, he came back out. "Got it. Tom Schmidt rented the car."

A tight ball of fear formed in Jake's gut. Was she taking Cassie to Tom? "Frank, I don't trust her. She may hurt Cassie."

Frank nodded. "We'll stop her. Don't worry."

Maggie bought coffees from the vending machine and handed him one. It tasted like mud, but he drank it anyway.

Twenty minutes ticked by before Frank opened the door, and his expression made Jake freeze.

"Jake, I'm sorry . . . There's been an accident."

"Are they all right?"

"The car went off the highway—a fifty-meter drop. It caught fire when it hit. No one could have survived."

No way. This wasn't how things ended for Cassie. "You're lying. It's not true!"

A pained looked crossed Frank's face. "I wish I were. Jake, emergency crews are there. They'll report back, but believe me—no one could have survived. The car had almost burned up by the time it extinguished itself in the river."

"Where are they?"

"Just this side of Pinton."

Anger flared in his chest. "Was she being chased? Was there a police vehicle following them?"

"No. I had units waiting for them right around the next corner. There's no way Jasmine could have known we were there."

"That highway has cement barricades."

Frank hesitated before speaking. "There were no skid marks. It looks like she accelerated and knocked the barricade away."

"Suicide?"

Frank looked like he didn't want to say it. "It's not conclusive, but yes."

"No. No, no, no!" Jake could hear himself screaming, but it sounded like it was coming from far away.

Frank put a hand on his shoulder. "I'm sorry."

Jake burst into tears.

Tears flowed down Maggie's cheeks. This was a nightmare. She just needed to wake up. Jake sat beside her, head in his hands, racked by sobs. She couldn't comfort him. His wife had just killed their only child. Susie was dead. *No one could have survived.* The words played in her mind, and she covered her ears as if it might block them out.

Suddenly, Chief MacKenzie burst through the door. "We've got Cassie. She's alive!"

Jake jumped up. "How badly is she hurt?"

"She's not. A woman called the Pinton RCMP to report a child and a dog abandoned outside her restaurant. They didn't put the two incidents together until now. Come on. They're waiting for you."

Jake rode in the front of the police cruiser, Maggie in the back. Frank put on the lights and siren. Finally, they pulled into the parking lot of the Pinton Springs Restaurant. Jake jumped out and raced inside. Maggie entered to find him with Cassie in his arms, Susie by his side.

Maggie rubbed Cassie's back. "Hi there."

"Hi." Cassie's face was pale, her eyes big.

Frank turned to the restaurant owner. "Can you tell me what happened?"

She pointed to the front window. "I was over there when I spotted them—the car was driving away. I ran out and brought them in. Cassie told me that the woman in the car was her mother. I called the police right away, because no mother in her right mind would leave a child on the side of the highway like that."

"Thank you," Jake said.

"Would you like some coffee?" the woman asked.

Jake shook his head. "No thanks. I think we'd better get Cassie home."

Chapter 36

[handwritten margin note: emergency landing / white knuckle landing]

JASMINE'S BODY WAS RECOVERED THE FOLLOWING MORNING.

Maggie sat on the bed, white-knuckling the phone. "How did Marie take it?"

[handwritten note: causing fear, apprehension, or panic.]

"She was hysterical," Jake said. "She's flying up tomorrow."

"And Cassie?"

"She's barely talking or eating. I asked her what happened, and she says she doesn't know."

"Shock?"

"I think so. I've got to go and identify the body. Cassie refuses to go to Sandra's. Could you come over?"

"Sure."

She clicked off the phone. The kitchen was a mess, the spaghetti sauce still in the frying pan, salad ingredients left out on the counter. How she'd slept at all she'd never understand, but somehow she'd staggered into bed late and passed out with relief. She looked at the unmade bed. It was all going to have to wait. Jake needed her, and the thought of him having to identify the body made her almost sick.

Twenty minutes later, Maggie arrived at the house and Jake greeted her with a long hug. They stepped inside, and he nodded toward the living room. "Cassie, I'm going now. Maggie's here."

Cassie looked over but didn't respond. He put his hands on his hips, observing his daughter.

"Don't worry. I'll take care of her."

He met her eyes. "Thanks."

She sat beside Cassie who was staring out the window with Susie's head resting on her knee. Cassie's hands didn't move to pet the dog. It looked like she'd completely shut down.

Maggie gently tapped Cassie's leg. "Come on. We've got to take Susie out."

They walked down to the beach. The day was overcast and threatening rain. At the water, Susie began to bark and jump back and forth. Maggie picked up a stick and threw it. Susie swam out, retrieved the stick and placed it at Cassie's feet.

"You throw it," Maggie said.

Cassie threw the stick. Susie returned, and Cassie tossed it again. No smiles, no giggles. She'd become robotic in her movements.

Maggie motioned to a log. "Let's sit."

Cassie stared straight ahead. Her face was pale, her eyes in a distant place.

"I know that yesterday was scary. You can talk about it when you're ready."

"Jasmine died," Cassie finally whispered.

Maggie slowly nodded. "I know, honey."

"Susie was hurt. We had to take her to the vet."

"Then what happened?"

Cassie turned, intense pain on her face. "Jasmine said Susie looked better, so we were going to meet my grandpa. I didn't want to go. I started to cry. She stopped the car. She said 'Get out,' but I couldn't get out."

"Why?"

"I couldn't move."

"You mean you were scared?"

Cassie nodded. "Jasmine opened the door and Susie ran away. I had to get Susie, but when I turned around, she was gone." Cassie started to cry.

"You mean your mom was gone."

"Yeah."

"And the lady at the restaurant came out and got you."

Cassie nodded as tears streamed down her cheeks.

Maggie pulled Cassie close as it started to rain. "Come on. Let's go inside."

As they made their way up the path, thunder rumbled and it began to pour.

Maggie closed the door against the elements, pulled off her wet cardigan, and put on the kettle. "Go change out of your wet clothes, and I'll make us hot chocolate. Maybe we can play a board game. You can pick one from the shelf in your room."

A few minutes later, Cassie came out wearing fresh clothes and carrying the *Candy Land* game.

"Set it up in the living room," Maggie said. "I'll just be a minute." She retrieved Cassie's wet clothes from the bedroom floor and took them to the laundry room. She hung the jeans on the drying rack. As she hung up Cassie's hooded sweat jacket, a paper fell out of the pocket. She unfolded it, expecting to see a piece of child's artwork.

It was a note.

Mom, I remember. Take care of Cassie.

Love you. Jas.

Maggie leaned on the washing machine, her heart pounding. After taking a few deep breaths, she walked out. Cassie had the game all set up. "I found this in the pocket of your jacket. Did your mom put it there?"

Cassie furrowed her brow. "Yeah. I forgot."

"When did she give it to you?"

"After she stopped the car. She wrote something and told me to put it in my pocket. Then she said, 'Get out, please get out—I can't do this anymore.' What is it?"

"It's a note to your grandma."

"We'd better give it to Grandma, then."

Maggie tucked the note into her pocket and forced herself to play the game. So Jasmine hadn't been ordering her daughter to get out. She'd been begging her to.

When Jake came home, he was white as a sheet. He shook his head. "Marie can't see Jasmine—not like that." He took out a bottle of whiskey, poured himself a shot, and downed it. He looked like a man about to break from stress.

Maggie told him what Cassie had said and showed him the note.

Jake shook his head. "My God. Do you think Jasmine remembered what Tom did to her?"

"She must have. Cassie said Jasmine was taking her to meet her grandfather. It must have all come back to her when Cassie started to cry." Maggie shook her head. "If Susie hadn't jumped out when she did, I wonder what would have happened."

Jake refilled his glass. "Maybe Susie knew Cassie was in trouble."

Maggie glanced into the living room. Cassie had her arm around the dog. "Maybe she did."

A knock sounded. Jake got up and answered it.

Mark stood in the rain, his coat pulled up over his head. "I thought you might need some company."

"He does," Maggie said. "Cassie and I are going to play a game and let you guys talk."

Chapter 37

THE FUNERAL WAS HELD ON THE LABOR DAY LONG WEEKEND. Kyle was waiting for Maggie at the church. They stepped inside and made themselves a pot of coffee then went to work spreading the sandwich fillings on bread.

Maggie went to the car and returned with the trays of baking they'd been working on all week. "I appreciate you helping me."

Kyle eyed the pastries and tarts. "No problem. Besides, I liked learning how to make all this."

A group arrived to set up the tables, and Connie and Charlene filed in with yellow roses to decorate.

Maggie and Kyle slipped into the sanctuary just as the organist began to play. Jake, Marie, and Cassie came down the aisle. Marie was crying, and Cassie looked wide-eyed.

Mark stepped to the front and bowed his head. "We remember, oh Lord, your child, Jasmine, and take comfort in the fact that she is now experiencing the joy and peace of Heaven. We commit her soul to you."

A hymn was sung then Mark took the pulpit to give the eulogy.

"Jasmine was a happy and contented baby. As a child, she liked to spend time outdoors playing with friends or swinging on the tire swing that hung from a thick branch of the apple tree in their backyard. Jasmine often picked her mother's flowers, and although the bouquet consisted of mismatched lengths, leaving bare spots in Marie's prized garden, Marie never told Jasmine to do otherwise. How could she when she saw the loving look on her daughter's face?"

Maggie glanced at her watch and signaled to Kyle that they had to go.

Kyle took out the platters of food, while Maggie made the tea and laid out the cream and sugar. She followed Kyle outside. Although it had been overcast, the clouds had cleared, and she was glad that on such an emotionally dismal day the weather was at least favorable. The food stretched out on a long buffet table. People hadn't known Jasmine well, but they'd come out in droves to support Jake, Cassie, and Marie.

The doors of the church opened. Jake, Marie, and Cassie walked out and stopped to form a line. Cassie looked uncomfortable as people hugged her and took her hand. Marie looked relieved and almost peaceful. Jake stood strong, meeting people's eyes, shaking hands and occasionally letting one hand drift to Cassie's shoulder.

As people helped themselves to coffee and food, Jake walked over with his parents and his sister, who had traveled down from Beaver Lake.

"Maggie, I'd like you to meet my mom and dad, Marcy and Russ. He threw an arm around his sister, who was tall and slim with straight brown hair and the same blue eyes as Jake. "And this is Shelby."

Maggie shook each of their hands.

"It was a touching service," Marcy said. She glanced at the tables. "Did you prepare all this food?"

"Kyle helped." Kyle, hearing his name, glanced over. He looked older than his age in a pair of black pants and a white dress shirt. If she wasn't mistaken, he and Shelby had just shared a look. She introduced them, and within moments, they were exchanging Facebook addresses. They walked away, their phones in their hands. Cassie ran by, chased by Rose. Marcy grabbed the two of them. "Slow down, you two."

"Thanks, Mom." Jake turned to Cassie. "Listen to your grandma, all right?"

Cassie nodded.

"I should make the rounds."

As he walked away, Russ—an older version of Jake—met Maggie's eyes. "I hear you and Jake had a few adventures this summer."

Her cheeks grew warm. His son had risked his life to save her from a guy she never should have gotten involved with. "We have."

"So you were in the witness protection program?"

"Russ!" Marcy said. "That's personal."

"That's all right," Maggie said. "It wasn't exactly witness protection. That's where you get a whole new identity. I just had to lie low, because I didn't trust the police to protect me in Vancouver."

"Ah—a duck and cover operation." Russ turned to the food table. "I'm going to get me some eats."

"Nice meeting you," Marcy said and hurried away after her husband.

Maggie wasn't hungry. She saw Marie standing alone and walked over. "I'm sorry for your loss."

"Thank you, Maggie." She waved a hand over the buffet table. "And thank you for preparing all this."

"You're welcome."

Marie glanced at the roses and started to cry. "Yellow roses were her favorites." She took the tissue Maggie offered. "I saw the note. It meant everything to me. Jasmine did love me. I know that now. If you hadn't found that note, Jake may have washed the jacket, and it would have been destroyed." She shook her head. "I might never have known what went through her mind in those final moments."

Maggie motioned to some chairs. "Let's sit."

Marie nodded gratefully. Then she froze. "Oh my God. Tom!"

Maggie whirled around. An overweight, balding man was down on one knee, talking to Cassie. Marie clutched the back of the chair like she was about to faint.

"Your ex-husband?" Maggie asked.

Marie nodded.

Maggie sprinted over. Tom looked up, spotted her, and yanked Cassie toward the parking lot. Cassie pulled back and screamed. Maggie grabbed Tom by the arm. "Let her go!"

Jake whirled around at the sound of Cassie's scream. Tom had Cassie in an iron grip, and Maggie was clawing at his arm. Jake was there in seconds, launching himself into a full-body tackle. *Thud.* Tom fell on his back. Jake used his forearm to lean on Tom's throat and glanced around. Maggie had Cassie in her arms. They were safe.

When he looked back, Tom had pulled out a gun. *Shit.* Jake grabbed Tom's arm and the gun fired into the air. He pounded Tom's arm against the ground until the gun fell.

"She's my granddaughter," Tom yelled. "Jasmine wanted me to have her."

Jake leaned on Tom's neck. "I'll kill you, you bastard, you son of a bitch." He thought about what this man had done to Jasmine, and what he wanted to do to Cassie. He leaned in harder until Tom's face turned red and his eyes bulged. "Can't think? Can't breathe? What do you think your actions did to her? They killed her!" Jake clenched his fist and pulled back his arm.

Someone grabbed his arm from behind. "Jake, don't." It was his father's voice. "Let the police take care of it. Cassie is watching."

Jake turned his head and saw the terrified expression on Cassie's face. He lowered his fist. A number of men jumped on Tom. Jake got up and dusted himself off. Ed took a linen napkin and retrieved the gun.

Mark came over and put a hand on Jake's shoulder. "The police are on the way."

Jake picked up Cassie. "Sorry, pumpkin. I didn't mean to scare you. That man is a very bad man."

"I didn't get in the car, Daddy." Cassie started to cry. "I was a good girl."

Jake pulled Cassie close. "So you knew he was a stranger. Smart girl. I'm proud of you."

Sirens announced the arrival of the police.

Chief Frank MacKenzie assessed the situation and pulled out his gun. "Let him go." The men released Tom and he clambered to his feet. "Put your hands on your head."

"I'm going to sue for assault," Tom spluttered.

Ed handed Tom's gun to one of the officers. "He drew a weapon and fired a shot. Jake disarmed him before anyone was hurt."

Frank nodded. "Read him his rights."

Tom was put in one of the police cruisers and taken away.

Two officers stayed behind to take statements. When they'd finished interviewing Jake, Maggie came over and put her hand on his arm. "Could you please tell people to stay and eat? I don't want it to end like this. Tom can't have the final word." She sighed. "Look at poor Marie."

Jake scanned the crowd. Marie sat with Connie to her right and Charlene to her left. The two women looked like they were trying to comfort her. Gabriela stood alone, crossing herself and praying. Other people huddled in groups, talking in hushed tones.

Jake called for everyone's attention. "Everything has been taken care of. Please, stay and have some food."

People slowly approached the tables. His mother came and took Cassie's hand. "Come on, sweetie. Let's get some juice."

"I can't believe Tom had the nerve to show up here," Maggie said.

Jake shook his head. "Me neither."

"Should we set an example and try some of this food that I spent all week making?"

"Sounds good."

As they helped themselves to sandwiches and pastries, Russ walked over, munching on a carrot stick. "How about you two come for a little trip to Beaver Lake? Looks like you both could use a holiday."

Jake poured a cup of coffee. "We'll think about that. By the way, Dad, thanks for stopping me back there."

"No problem. But you should know: if Cassie hadn't been watching, I would have helped you beat the crap out of him."

Chapter
38

Tom held Cassie down on the ground with his hands around her throat. No, it wasn't Cassie—it was Jasmine he held down. Jake glanced at Tom's hands—the left hand wore Jake's wedding ring. They were not Tom's hands after all; they were his own. He was killing her. What had he done?

Jake sat up with a start and turned on the lamp. The dream seemed so real. He glanced over at his bedside clock—3:00 a.m. He needed to get up and move around. If he went back to sleep, he might return to the nightmare. He threw on a robe and headed to the kitchen. He needed something stronger than milk. He pulled out a bottle of whiskey and poured himself a shot.

He sat in the living room. He'd had about all he could take. Marie had gone to stay at Charlene's house. Charlene had lost a niece to suicide, and the two women had made some kind of connection. *Good.* It was hard to look at Marie when he'd killed her daughter.

Where had that come from?

He took another sip of whiskey, feeling it burn his throat but warm his insides. Jasmine had just been served the divorce papers when she'd taken Cassie. She'd also just lost custody. He should have known how unstable she was. He'd pushed her right off a cliff.

He'd wanted to set a boundary. Well, death was a pretty big boundary. And she'd almost taken Cassie with her. He could have lost his daughter, all because he'd been so damn eager to get on with his own life.

He walked out to the deck. Full moon, stars, the river a glimmering phantom under the shadow of the hills. He could have saved her, insisted on counseling, dragged her to a doctor—anything but hit her with divorce papers. At one point in his marriage, Jasmine had asked him to move back to Vancouver. He'd refused because of business. Business! There were psychiatrists in the city. She could have gotten help. If only he could go back and change one thing to make the outcome different.

He stepped inside and rinsed out his glass. He'd messed up once. He wasn't going to mess up again. Maggie had been traumatized by the incident with Carlo. It showed in her eyes and in the way she startled at everything. He could ask her to stay, but not in the condition she was in. It wouldn't be fair. She could meet an unencumbered man and have a family of her own. She didn't need this. She didn't need him. She might think she did, but she'd be way better off without him.

Maggie and Kyle stood side by side, companionably rolling out pastry. Maggie used the back of her hand to push a lock of hair off her forehead. "I'll never understand why Maynard doesn't open this place for dinner."

"Me neither. Not everybody wants to eat Chinese food when they go out."

"He could serve a whole different menu at night."

Kyle glanced over. "Even bring in local musicians."

"Hey, you two, there are orders here," Lily called out.

Maggie yanked the orders off the order wheel. Best to keep busy. She didn't want to think about Tom showing up at the funeral. It made her hands shake.

Lily took a complimentary tray of swan-shaped cream puffs around to the customers. Kyle and Maggie huddled at the pass-through window to watch. A rancher, his cowboy hat on the table, held the delicate pastry between his large, work-worn thumb and middle finger and turned it around and around. Finally, he popped the whole thing in his mouth, lifted his eyebrows then ran his tongue over his lips, as if trying to find another crumb. Maggie and Kyle exchanged a smile. *Success.*

Jake and Cassie walked in. Jake looked exhausted, and Cassie had a lopsided ponytail that she'd obviously done herself. Lily held out the tray and Cassie took a pastry.

Maggie pushed through the swinging doors. "Hey, you guys."

"Hi," Jake said.

She sat them at a table near the wall. Jake seemed different, aloof. But what did she expect? His wife had been buried the day before. "What can I get for you?"

Cassie smiled. "Pancakes."

Jake glanced at Cassie. "You want pancakes for lunch?"

She nodded.

He handed the menus to Maggie. "I'll have the clubhouse. Salad, no fries."

Maggie returned to the kitchen. She mixed up the pancake batter, and on a whim, made one large pancake in the shape of a C.

She delivered it to Cassie. "Do you know what it is?"

"The letter C!"

"For?"

"Cassie!"

Jake stared at the pancake without a trace of amusement.

Maggie placed the clubhouse sandwich in front of him. Maybe he was still shell-shocked from all the events of the day before. She struggled to make conversation. "So . . . it's September. I'm going to have to figure out what to do. Either pay the rent on my Vancouver apartment or let it go."

He looked up. "You miss the city?"

"A little."

He stared at her. "Because if that's where you want to be, I think you should go."

Was he trying to get rid of her? "I've been a little on the fence about moving."

He shrugged and looked at his sandwich. "Summer's almost over. No sense waiting around."

Got it. He was trying to get rid of her. "Anything else?"

"No thanks." She felt dismissed.

She walked back to the kitchen and leaned her forehead against the fridge.

"Hey, Maggie, you OK?" Kyle asked.

"Sure." Less than two weeks ago, she'd been snuggling in bed with Jake. What had changed?

And then suddenly, it hit her.

Jake blamed her. If she'd been watching Cassie more carefully, Jasmine wouldn't have been able to abduct her. None of this would have happened. *The funeral.* That's when he'd changed. That's when he'd decided she'd be a lousy person to have around his daughter.

Kyle pulled the croissants out of the oven. "They turned out great."

Maggie stared at the pastry. What the heck was she doing hanging around here? Her leg had healed. Even her emotions had come a long way with Beatrice's help. What was holding her? Nothing. Not anymore. "Kyle, I'm moving back to Vancouver."

Kyle's face fell. "When did you decide that?"

"Recently. If you ever need a reference, I'd be happy to give it." She grabbed some orders off the wheel and busied herself at the grill. When she next looked out, Jake was heading to the till. If he wanted to get rid of her, it was time to let him know she was already going. She straightened her back and walked out.

She rang in the bill and handed him the change. "Actually, I'm leaving in a week. You're right—there's no point in sitting on the fence. The tourist season is pretty much over. Maynard doesn't need me anymore. It's time I got back to Vancouver and on with my life."

For half a second, she thought he looked hurt, but then he nodded, his eyes serious. "You'll be glad you did."

Cassie stared up at her, and Maggie wanted to burst into tears.

Jake took Cassie's hand. "Bye," was all he said.

After they left, Lily strolled over, coffeepot in hand. "You're really leaving?"

"Yes."

"Me too. I'm going to Kamloops. The college sent my acceptance letter a few weeks ago."

Maggie forced a smile. "That's wonderful!"

"Rose and I will be back in a year. Maybe you'll be back, too."

Maggie shook her head. "I don't think so."

Lily bit her lip and took a moment before speaking. "Jake's been through a lot. Give him time."

Maggie glanced out the window, hoping that Jake would run back in and tell her it was a big mistake. Tell her he loved her. But that wasn't going to happen, so she might as well face the facts. She turned to Lily. "He blames me for what happened. That's not going away."

"What do you mean?"

"I was the one babysitting when Cassie was taken. Would you want someone like that in Rose's life?"

Lily knit her brow. "But Jasmine was waiting for her. I mean, we put six-year-olds out to play. No one could have foreseen that."

A wave of depression hit her. "I'm pretty sure he doesn't see it that way."

Lily hugged her. "I'm going to miss you."

Maggie returned the hug. "I'll miss you too."

So this was how her little venture to Rosetown ended. *Crap.* She'd grown to like the place.

Chapter 39

"I THINK I HAVE STOCKHOLM SYNDROME," MAGGIE SAID. SHE glanced at the basket of dried sage in the corner of Beatrice's office. According to First Nation lore, it held healing properties. She breathed in the sweet, musty smell. *Nope.* It wasn't doing much for her right now.

Beatrice reached out and touched Maggie's hand, something she'd never done before. When Maggie looked up, Beatrice smiled. "How so?"

"This town captured me, and I fell in love with it."

Beatrice furrowed her brow like she didn't understand.

Maggie felt herself deflate. "I know. The syndrome is about falling in love with a human captor . . . but in a way, I've been so isolated and traumatized that I don't want to leave Rosetown. Maybe I've even fallen in love with Jake in some misguided way. He was the hero who saved me. There's got to be some kind of syndrome for that." She shrugged. "Anyway, it doesn't matter. He's not having much to do with me anymore."

"Jake's been through a lot. He just lost his wife. I know they weren't together, but it would still be hard on him."

"I know that." Maggie did know that, but she hated the way he'd practically ordered her out of his life. "What I don't get is how Jasmine could suddenly remember she was abused and the next second think that driving off a cliff was her only option."

Beatrice leaned back, her head cocked to one side. "It's not that Jasmine didn't remember. She'd just repressed the memory."

"But she was taking Cassie to her father—the man who abused her."

"It happens. Sometimes a woman grows up with an abusive father and goes on to marry an abusive man. Why?"

Maggie tilted her head. "Because it's familiar?"

"Yes. Or she is still trying to come to terms with the primary relationship."

"So you think that on some level Jasmine was trying to remember by taking Cassie to Tom?"

"Possibly. Unfortunately, when the memory came back, she didn't have anyone there with her." Beatrice paused. "It would have taken every ounce of her energy to stop the car and tell Cassie to get out."

Somewhere in her gut, Maggie understood. Look at how much of her relationship with Carlo she'd buried. If she hadn't had these counseling sessions, it may never have come out. "So Jasmine wanted to protect Cassie. Maybe she even loved her?"

Beatrice nodded. "I think she did."

Maggie glanced at her watch. "I know my time's not up, but I think I'm ready." She stood and looked out the window. "It's a beautiful day. I'm going for a walk."

"Could I join you?" Beatrice asked.

Maggie was taken aback. "Sure."

Beatrice smiled. "I know it would never happen in the city, but this is Rosetown, and if I want to go for a walk with a client, I go for a walk."

"Great. Let's go."

They followed the river path, talking about Maggie's plans for the future. *Job as a chef. Nice restaurant. Friends of her own who weren't associated with Carlo.* It sounded hollow even to her own ears. They came to the little park by the museum and sat on the wooden bench.

"Look at this view," Maggie said. "I can't believe I'm going back to traffic and crowds."

"You're going back to sort things out and gain perspective." Beatrice folded her hands in her lap and gazed at the water. "When I was a little girl, my grandmother shared a belief that my people hold. She told me that if I whispered my secrets to the river, the river would take those secrets and reach the sea with them. When the water reached the sea, I would be free from those secrets."

"That's beautiful."

"Sometimes when my clients can't tell me something because of the shame involved, I suggest this. After they tell the river, they come back and find it easier to speak to me."

Maggie shook her head. "It must be hard to do what you do."

"Yes. Almost impossible at times. I hear the stories—children stolen from their homes, stolen from their culture, abused, hit for speaking their own language—and I think I can't hear anymore." Beatrice paused. "But if the river can hear it, so can I. I let myself be the river. I let it go into my brain, through my heart, and back out to sea. I don't hold onto it." Beatrice slowly rubbed her knees before getting to her feet. "Gosh, I'm starting to sound like a hokey old elder. Time for me to get back to work."

Maggie hugged her. "Thank you. You've really helped me."

"You're welcome. Give me a call sometime. Tell me how you're making out."

"I'll do that."

Jake paced up and down the beach like a caged animal. Cassie was at school, and every fiber of his being wanted to call Maggie and beg her to stay. He stared at the phone. Just one push of a button—that's all he had to do. He pulled back his arm and winged the phone into the river. He hopped into his boat and started the engine. He leapt over the waves and tried to forget what it was like to hold Maggie in his arms. If he didn't talk to someone, he was going to lose it.

He pulled up at the dock, jogged up the trail, and pounded on the church door. After a moment, he hammered again.

Mark came out from the rectory next door. "Jake, my man. What's up?"

Jake let out his breath and met his friend's eyes.

"Come in. We'll talk," Mark said.

Jake stepped into the house, so agitated that he wanted to punch a wall. "It's Maggie. She's leaving."

Mark put on the kettle and signaled for him to sit down. "She's going back to Vancouver?"

"Yeah."

Mark sat across from him. "And you want her to stay?"

Jake pushed a hand through his hair. "Exactly."

"Have you asked her?"

"No. Even if I could convince her, she's been so upset since Carlo showed up that I'd be taking advantage. Besides, I have Cassie to think about. I became an instant parent. I don't want to do that to Maggie. She can go Vancouver, meet an unencumbered man and have a family of her own someday."

The kettle whistled, and Mark got up to make the tea. "You could at least talk to her."

Jake thought about Jasmine, how he'd convinced her to move to Rosetown and she'd hated it. He'd taken Jasmine's life by trying to get what he wanted—a divorce. He'd been a selfish son of a gun, and he wasn't going to make the same mistake twice. "No, it's a bad idea. Maggie has a dream to go back and open her own restaurant."

Mark poured the tea. "If you want different things out of life, then you're incompatible."

"I guess so."

"So if you really love her, you'll let her go."

"It's killing me."

"Who said love was easy?"

Mark was right. "I won't call her."

"Good."

Mark pushed Jake's teacup toward him. "If you change your mind . . ."

Jake cut him off. "Don't worry. I won't."

"You're sure about that?"

"I threw my phone in the river."

Chapter 40

MAGGIE FOLDED HER CLOTHES AND PACKED THEM NEATLY into her suitcases. She'd said her goodbyes to most people, but she couldn't bring herself to call Jake. Not when he'd hurt her so badly. Since the day he'd told her to go, he hadn't called once. He hadn't even come into the restaurant. She was contemplating making one quick call just to say goodbye when a knock sounded.

Jake stood on the porch with Cassie, a bouquet of red roses in his hands. "We heard that you were leaving tomorrow. I know you can't take these with you, but you can at least enjoy them for a day." He handed her the flowers.

She smelled them. "Thank you. Roses to remind me of Rosetown."

Cassie handed her a paper. It was a drawing of a stick woman in a triangular yellow dress with a swirl of orange hair and a little girl with black curly hair. Beside them was a fat pink pig made of two circles, two eyes, and a snout. All three had large smiles. A bright yellow sun shone in the corner. It was signed *Cassie* in large print. "It's you, me, and Arnold."

"I can tell that. Thank you." Maggie gave Cassie a hug. "How's school?"

"Good. Can we make Arnold more biscuits?"

Jake raised his brows.

Maggie met his eyes. "We made biscuits when you were away in Edmonton. Arnold loved them, didn't he Cassie?"

She nodded.

Jake glanced at the open suitcases in the bedroom and turned to Cassie. "Maggie's busy. She doesn't have time."

Maggie placed her hands on her hips. *Really?* She didn't have time, or did he just want to hightail it out of there? "I've got time if you do," she challenged.

He relaxed his stance. "Sure."

She dragged a chair over to the counter and Cassie climbed up. "Do you need help?" Jake asked.

"You can keep us company." She nodded toward a kitchen chair.

He sat down. "Sounds good to me."

She and Cassie went to work, stirring and mixing. Cassie took a nibble of dough. "Cassie, remember what I told you. Cooks don't put their fingers in their mouths and then back into the batter."

"Do you think Arnold will mind?" Jake asked.

She glanced at him. "You'll mind when Cassie cooks for you!"

He laughed.

She'd missed that chuckle.

As Cassie used an upside-down glass to cut out the biscuits, Maggie scooped them up and put them on a tray. After placing the tray in the oven, she poured them each a glass of orange juice. As they sat around the kitchen table, a warm breeze blew in, and Maggie wanted the moment to last forever.

"Cassie, are you going to let us eat any, or are they all for Arnold?" Jake asked.

Cassie tipped her head. "Mostly for Arnold."

"How's Marie?" Maggie asked.

His face became serious. "Back in Vancouver doing more chemo."

Maggie shook her head. There was so much she wanted to say to him, but what was the point? Bottom line: he was no longer interested. They talked a little more about the weather and when the rafting season would end. She was almost relieved when the timer went off.

Cassie jumped off her chair. "They're done!"

Maggie held her back from the hot oven. "I'll get them."

They walked around to the back of the motel. Arnold lifted his nose and trotted over. Cassie climbed on the lowest rail of the fence and fed him a biscuit, then another and another.

Maggie kept her voice low so that Cassie wouldn't hear. "Any word on Tom?"

"Yeah. I talked to Frank. Tom's been shipped to Vancouver to face multiple charges: possession of a restricted and unregistered firearm, discharge of a firearm, and using it in a threatening manner. He'll do a minimum of three years' time if convicted of all three."

"Thank God. He'll never have access to Cassie now."

They were interrupted by Cassie hopping down from the fence and running over. "I left some for us," she said.

"You and your dad can have those. I should really get back to packing." Maggie could pack the rest of her things in five minutes if she wanted to, but there seemed no point in prolonging their goodbye.

Jake put a hand on Cassie's shoulder. "Time to say goodbye."

Maggie crouched down and hugged Cassie, who felt little-girl soft. She fought the lump in her throat.

"Daddy doesn't know how to make biscuits," Cassie said in a muffled voice.

EnglishClass101.com

Sounds fantastic
What do you call this? name this,

"Your grandma will be here soon, and she'll know how." Maggie stood and adjusted her face to conceal how much she was hurting. "Bye, Jake."

He hugged her and let go. "I'll call you sometime."

"Sure."

She waved as they drove away. It felt like someone had reached down and chopped out a whole chunk of her heart.

Jeannie walked over. "We're going to miss you, love."

She turned. "I'm going to miss you too. I'm going to miss everything." Then she started to cry.

keep going
deep open question.
did you hear about it?
compliment to other persons
good conversation starter.

Don't afraid to open up.
How's it going? your life going.
What have you up to?
    doing since last time I saw you.
I've been sleeping a lot.
Do you wanna to type?
    want to

Chapter 41

MAGGIE'S VANCOUVER APARTMENT LOOKED LIKE A TORNADO had struck. Carlo and his friends had emptied every drawer and cupboard looking for the jewelry. Maggie opened the sliding door and stepped out onto the balcony. Reaching up to the overhanging ledge, she pulled down the small Tupperware container. She took out the emerald necklace, earrings, and bracelet. She'd never really liked them. There were way too many gemstones on each piece. But if Carlo had wanted them back, they were likely worth something.

She began to tidy up, and when everything was in place, she opened her laptop and searched for restaurants to apply to. She marked a few as favorites then switched to Facebook. Most of her contacts were in Calgary. Carlo had always been sulky when she wanted go out with her chef school friends. And he'd been downright rude to her brother when he visited.

An abusive relationship. That's what Beatrice had labeled it. He'd isolated her so he could control her. She slammed shut the laptop. She was older and wiser now. It would never happen again. First things first—get rid of anything associated with Carlo. She put the jewelry in her purse and took the elevator down to street level, where she waited for the bus. Everyone was fiddling with their phones. No one looked up to smile or comment on the weather. This was her life now. She might as well get used to it.

She got off at Linden's Jewelers, walked through the glass doors and was greeted by a woman wearing a black skirt and a pink silk blouse, her hair pulled back into a sleek bun. "May I help you?" the woman asked.

Feeling out of place in her faded jeans and Converse runners, Maggie opened the Tupperware container. "I'd like to have these pieces assessed."

The woman's mouth fell open before she quickly composed herself. She passed Maggie a form. "Sign here, please. The assessor will need thirty minutes."

Maggie went next door and ordered a coffee. People around her chatted or worked on their laptops. She didn't know anyone. Rosetown felt like a dream, a bubble. Maybe with time, it would burst. It had to. She didn't like feeling that her body was in one place and her heart in another.

When she returned to the jewelry store, the sales clerk greeted her with a smile. She handed Maggie the Tupperware container. "They're exquisite pieces. Colombian emeralds—the best in the world. Are you thinking of selling?"

"Yes."

"I'm authorized to offer you forty thousand, but I'm sure you'll want to think about it. Here's our card."

Maggie walked out of the shop in a state of disbelief. She found a green space and sat on a park bench. Then it hit her— forty thousand dollars. That was enough to plan out the rest of her life. She could pick and choose where she wanted to work. Then her conscience kicked in. She couldn't sell the jewelry, not if it was considered the proceeds of a crime. She took out her phone and scrolled through her contacts. Before she could think too hard about what she was giving up, she pressed the call button.

"Vancouver Police. Sheraton here."

"It's Maggie Jackson."

"Ah. Didn't I make it clear to Chief MacKenzie that you were under no obligation to us anymore?"

"It's not that." She explained the situation. "I think the jewelry was Carlo's way of getting his money out of Columbia."

"And he gifted it to you?"

"Yes, but he asked for it back." She described how he'd threatened her.

She could almost hear him shaking his head. "Look, Carlo's dead, and we have no jurisdiction over Colombia. If he gave it to you, it's yours. Anything else?"

"No."

"Bye." He clicked off the phone.

She looked at the phone. He was the same brusque man that she remembered.

Suddenly everything looked brighter. She walked down to the ocean. Sailboats, freighters, seagulls—the city was a great place. A panhandler wearing dirty clothes and a pitiful expression approached her. "Could you help me out?" he asked.

She thought of the jewelry tucked in her purse and gave him a ten-dollar bill.

Cassie gave Jake a kiss, and she ran into the classroom after the other children. So this was his life now: single father, great little rafting business, and a hole in his heart the size of a crater.

"Jake!" someone called out.

"Oh. Hi, Tamara." She looked different in sweatpants and a ponytail, and she didn't smell like perfume.

"It's great to have them back at school, isn't it? Do you have time to go for coffee?"

"Sorry. I've got some things to do today."

"Another time, then."

"Sure." He was letting bygones be bygones. Tamara was harmless. She'd obviously just rolled out of bed to bring her son to school. She was doing the best she could, just like him.

Jake went to the grocery store and bought a bouquet of mixed flowers.

When he reached the cemetery, he stood and took in the view. Far below, the river snaked through a clay-colored canyon, and the fields had turned golden, dotted with wild baby's breath as far as the eye could see.

He walked past a worn teddy bear on a child-sized grave. If Jasmine hadn't put Cassie out of the car, he could be visiting two graves today. He placed the flowers in front of Jasmine's headstone. "I'm sorry. I should have been a better husband." Emotion welled up in his chest, and he was racked by a sudden sob. "God, Jasmine. Why did you do this?"

Someone called his name. Ed walked over and put a hand on his shoulder. "Hey, Jake."

"I didn't expect to see you here," Jake managed.

Ed met his eyes, his weathered face sad. "With Lily and Rose gone, the house is depressingly quiet. I thought I'd come and visit Sophie, tell her how her daughter is doing. Boy, she'd be proud to know that Lily's going to college and planning to set up her own business." He glanced at Jasmine's headstone. "It's tough."

Jake wiped away a tear with the back of his hand. *So stupid.* He hadn't cried when she died. He hadn't cried at the funeral. *Why now?* "I just wish I could have prevented it. Done something differently."

"We all feel that way," Ed said.

Jake shook his head. "No, you don't understand. I tried to get her help. So did Marie. But we didn't try hard enough."

Ed nodded. "Sometimes all the trying in the world isn't enough."

Suddenly Jake wanted to spill his guts. "I served her with divorce papers the day of the accident. I was just so damn impatient to get on with my life—to be a free man." There. It was out. He'd as good as killed her.

Ed furrowed his brow. "Seems to me people kill themselves because of something on the inside. Depression. Hopelessness. Despair. Not divorce papers."

Jake met Ed's eyes, wanting what he said to be true. "Maybe."

"You told me your wife was sexually abused as a child."

Jake nodded. "She was."

"I was abused as well." Ed sighed and shook his head. "I guess that's one of the reasons I tried to drink myself to death. When I started going to Alcoholics Anonymous, it was awful. It all came back. If I hadn't had the support of the group, I may have just taken my hunting rifle out to the bush and ended it." He paused. "What I'm saying is, I don't think Jasmine was running from divorce papers or even the fact that she'd lost custody of her daughter. I think she was running from something inside herself. Something so terrible that it was enough to make her drive right off a cliff."

Jake let Ed's words sink down inside, and suddenly, he was crying again. He looked at the headstone and thought of Jasmine's pain. It made sense. He hadn't killed her. The abuse had. He turned to Ed and wiped away the tears. "I think you're right."

They stood in silence for a few minutes, each lost in their own thoughts.

"Are you working today?" Ed finally asked.

"No."

"Feel like taking a drive to the fish camp? It's a good run this year."

Jake nodded, a weight lifted. "Yeah, I do."

"Just let me go say goodbye to Sophie."

As Ed walked away, Jake moved the flowers closer to the gravestone. A breeze stroked his brow, and he felt her—ethereal, but whole and full of joy. Somehow, she'd become perfect. "Go to God," he whispered. "I'll take care of things here."

Chapter 42

THE DAYS GREW CHILLIER AS SEPTEMBER GAVE WAY TO October. Maggie came in from her jog, showered, and drank a large glass of water. Time to get back to work. Her kitchen table was strewn with notes. She had to figure out if opening a restaurant was even feasible. So far, she'd been put off by the high price of Vancouver real estate. Commercial buildings sold for millions, and even leases ran upward of four thousand a month. It was down to two choices: either she could get a chef job and save for twenty years, or she could open up her own place in a small town.

She fired up her laptop. Rosetown—out of the question. Perhaps if she just moved to Maple Ridge or Abbotsford . . . Her cell phone buzzed.

"Maggie. It's Mark."

"Mark! How are you?"

"Fine. I'm in Vancouver, visiting my son. He's busy for the day. Any chance we could meet up?"

"I'd love to. Where are you?"

"Near the university."

"How about Earl's on Broadway?"

She closed the laptop, her heart pounding. *Mark*. That meant she'd hear about Jake. Did she want to hear about Jake? She put on makeup and earrings and stepped out the door.

When she entered the restaurant, Mark stood and waved her over. They hugged.

"Nice to see you again," Mark said.

"You too."

"So how's city life?"

"Great." A waitress poured them coffee.

Maggie told Mark about the jewelry, the money, and her desire to open her own restaurant.

"Where would you open this place?"

"A small town somewhere. I can't afford the city."

Mark spluttered on his coffee. "Small like Rosetown?"

"No, I can't go back there. I'd be stepping on Jake's toes."

"Why would you say that?"

"He thinks if I'd been watching Cassie more closely, Jasmine wouldn't have taken her."

Mark frowned. "Do you think that?"

"No. Of course not. I only took my eyes off Cassie for a few minutes, and she was with a group of children."

The waitress strolled over. They quickly opened their menus and ordered burgers. When the waitress walked away, Mark turned back to Maggie, a small crease between his eyes.

Her pulse quickened. "Mark, is Jake seeing someone?"

He sighed. "No, and he doesn't blame you, either. You couldn't have known that Jasmine was at the motel. I mean, who knows how long she'd been waiting there, hoping for an opportunity? She had it all planned right down to how to get Cassie into the car. Jake knows that."

"So why did he practically chase me out of town?"

Mark removed his glasses and rubbed them with a tissue. "I guess I'm going to have to do something that I never do."

"What's that?"

He put on his glasses. "Break a confidence."

Maggie straightened her back. "If you tell Jake what I said, I will kill you, pastor or no pastor."

Mark laughed. "I'm not going to break your confidence. I'm going to break his. You can do whatever you like with the information."

"Go on."

"Jake thought you'd been through so much that if he asked you to stay, he'd be taking advantage. He could see that you were still recovering from the ordeal with Carlo. He knew you liked the city, and he didn't want you to give up on your dreams and regret it later."

"Shouldn't that have been my choice?" She thought for a minute. "And who says my dreams are tied to the city anyway?"

Mark put up a hand. "Let me finish. He also thought you'd rather meet someone who didn't have a child. He became an instant father when he married. He didn't want to do the same to you."

"Cassie is the sweetest little girl in the world. Why wouldn't I want her?"

"When you put it that way, I can't think of a reason." Mark hesitated. "The thing is, when you were about to leave, Jake came to me. He was so distressed that he'd thrown his cell phone into the river just to keep himself from calling you, but I told him that if you wanted different things out of life, you were incompatible." A guilty expression played across Mark's face.

"What else?"

"I also said that if he loved you, he should let you go."

She rose and hit him over the head with a paper napkin. "What is wrong with you? After he organizes a whole rafting trip to get you and Gabriela together, you tell him to not call?"

"That's why he invited us out on the raft?"

"Duh."

Mark's shoulders sagged. "I'm going to make this right."

Maggie leaned forward. "No, you're not. I had to come back here anyway to figure out what I really wanted."

"You mean to own your own restaurant?"

"I always knew that. What I really want is to be with Jake and see if it works out. That way I don't have to wonder about what could have been for the rest of my life." Their burgers arrived. "Did he really throw his cell phone in the river?"

"He did."

"Mark, you're not going to say a word. I'll figure this out."

Mark smiled. "My lips are sealed, but Maggie . . ."

"Yes?"

"Hurry up. The poor guy is miserable."

Chapter 43

MAGGIE SAT AT THE KITCHEN TABLE, STARING AT HER laptop. The best solution was to open a restaurant in Lahara. While she searched for commercial space, she could work at Maynard's, if he'd still have her.

She closed the window to muffle the sounds from the street below and picked up the phone. "Hi, Maynard. It's Maggie."

There was a pause. "Maggie Jackson?"

"Yes. How are you?"

"Good."

Might as well cut to the chase. "Any chance I could have my job back?"

He didn't answer.

"Maynard, did you hear me?"

"Yeah, yeah, I heard. I was just thinking. Can't you let a man think?"

"Sorry." She held her breath.

"I just bought a cabin on one of my favorite fishing lakes. I've been looking all summer long for a place like this."

"So that's why you were taking the time off."

"Yeah. I'm retiring. I'm selling my house and the restaurant and moving out there. I've already listed them both."

Maggie's heart began to pound. "What's the restaurant listed for?"

"Two hundred fifty thousand. That's the business, the building, and the property."

She closed her eyes and dove in. "I can offer you two thirty."

"You want to buy it?" He sounded skeptical.

She paused for two seconds before replying. "I do."

"You got that kind of money?"

She thought of her newly replenished bank account. "I was practically married to the mob, remember?"

Maynard didn't laugh.

"Fine," she huffed. "I have a down payment. And I'll get a mortgage."

"Make it two forty, and it's yours."

"Two thirty-five."

"Done."

"I'll go to the bank today. Don't tell anyone. Agreed?"

"For a quick sale, my lips are sealed. By the way, a rancher was in the other day asking for one of those little swan pastries. You know anything about that?"

Maggie smiled. "Maybe." She hung up and called her parents. "Mom, remember my dream of opening up my own restaurant?"

"Yes."

"I think it's about to come true."

There was a crispness to the air, and it was one of the last days the congregation would be able to have their coffee outside. A barbecue was set up, and the smell of salmon filled the air.

Jake walked over to Mark. "How was the trip?"

"Good." Mark took a sip of coffee.

"Did you call Maggie?"

"Yes." Mark smiled at someone who walked by.

Jake tilted his head. "Did you get together?"

"Very briefly." A few people were setting salads on the buffet table. "Looks like I should say the blessing."

Mark wasn't getting off that easy. "How is she?"

"Fine."

Mark never answered in monosyllables. He was holding back. Two could play at this game. "Don't worry. I'm over her."

A look of distress crossed Mark's face. "You are?"

"Sure." Jake put his hands behind his back and waited.

"Look, I can't say what Maggie and I discussed. Just give her a call. *Please.*"

Jake's heart took a leap. "There's hope?"

"There's always hope. Call her and tell her how you feel."

Chapter 44

THE WHOLE WEEK WAS A FLURRY OF ACTIVITY AS THE mortgage was approved, the sales contract was signed, and the money was wired to Maynard. Maggie kept telling herself that if she didn't like owning the restaurant, she could sell it and move on. It was just a chapter in her life—she didn't know the end of the story.

The intercom buzzed. "Yes?"

"Diabetes Society."

"Come up."

Two burly men loaded all her furniture out of the apartment. She was donating everything except what could fit in the Plymouth.

She was just about to go out the door when her phone sounded. Call display showed it was Jake.

Her heart pounded. What if this was a huge mistake? "Hi."

"How are you?" he asked.

She sat on the floor, since she no longer owned any furniture. "Great. You?"

"Good. Did you get a job?" He didn't sound in love. He sounded like an old friend just calling to check up on her.

The balcony door was open, and the air was freezing. She pulled her sweater around her. "No, I'm planning on opening my own place."

"Congratulations. You thought that would be years away."

So Mark had stuck to his word and not told Jake about their conversation. "I came into some money. How's your business going?"

"I've finished the rafting season. I'm employed as an electrician for now, but I'm still working on the off-season tourism idea. It's just going to take some time. But I want to hear more about your restaurant."

She got up and closed the balcony door. "It's just a coffee shop. Nothing fancy." Below her, the street was lined with maple trees, their leaves bright red. People strolled along, some with dogs, others with babies in strollers. A few bikers whizzed by.

"What are you calling it?" Jake asked.

"Maggie's Restaurant."

He laughed. "Come on, you're making fun of us up here. What's the real name?"

She smiled. "I haven't decided. How's Cassie?"

"She's great. She likes first grade."

"And Marie?"

"She's moved to Rosetown. She bought a small house over on Second Street. Her health is improving, and between her and Sandra, I never have to worry about babysitting anymore."

"That's good." If he didn't say something soon, Maggie was going to feel like the biggest fool on the face of the planet.

"Sorry I didn't call earlier," he said. His voice sounded tender, and she could almost picture him standing in his living room looking out at the river. "I wanted to—there were things I wanted to tell you. I didn't want you to leave. I really . . ."

"Jake." She interrupted him. "I was just on my way out the door. Can I call you back?"

"Sure." He sounded disappointed.

"I'll talk to you tomorrow."

"OK."

"Bye." She clicked off the phone. She needed to have this conversation in person. Three suitcases and four boxes were piled by the door. It was time to drive out of town.

Chapter 45

WHEN SHE ARRIVED AT THE PONDEROSA MOTEL, THE courtyard was empty. Bob and Jeannie were taking a well-deserved break. Jeannie had stocked Maggie's unit with tea bags, coffee, and cream, so Maggie put on the kettle. It had been a long drive, but a beautiful one—the fall colors were spectacular. She made some chamomile tea and keyed in Maynard's number.

"You here?" Maynard asked.

"Just got in. Can you still meet me in the morning?"

"Yeah. I'd better get some shut-eye. Five o'clock rolls around pretty early."

She finished her tea and stepped outside. Hundreds of bright stars twinkled overhead, maybe even thousands. A few crickets hummed and nothing else. *Heaven.*

She walked around to Arnold's enclosure. "Arnold! Arnold!"

The pig came out. She pulled some parsnips from the garden and fed him. If all went well, she'd be back in a few days with Cassie and a bucket of biscuits.

She returned to her unit, crawled into bed, and willed herself to go to sleep.

The next morning, she parked in front of the restaurant. Maynard pulled up in his truck not five minutes later. They unloaded the ladders and drills, took down the *Maynard's* sign and replaced it with a large white awning decorated with beautifully painted flowers. In bold script, it announced *Maggie's Restaurant.*

As the sun rose, they stepped across the street to admire their work. Maggie took her car and parked it on a side street.

As she stepped into the restaurant, she looked at it with new eyes. Sure, it would stay a diner during the day, but at night she was going to transform it into a place where people could eat out in style, complete with candles, white linen, and fairy lights.

Maynard handed her a coffee and motioned for her to join him at a table. "Still don't know why you didn't just tell him you were coming back," he said. "He's been through enough already."

Maggie smiled. "Oh, so you like him now?"

"I like that little peanut he has with him."

"Cassie?"

He nodded.

Maggie tipped her head. "Why Maynard, I didn't know you liked children."

He shrugged. "Like 'em more than adults."

Maynard finished his coffee and walked through the swinging doors to the kitchen. Maggie turned the sign to *Open.*

Customers strolled in. They seemed pleased that the menu would stay the same, at least during daytime hours. Butterflies played in her stomach. What would she do if Jake didn't come by today?

Then she saw him. Jake stood outside, hands on his hips, just staring up at the sign. Her heart went *thump, thump, thump.* Realization dawned on his face. He pulled open the door, grabbed her up, and whirled her around, his blue eyes intense.

"You don't need to feel obligated," she said. "It was just an opportunity."

"Got it. No obligation." He kissed her.

"I mean . . . I could never afford to own my own place in the city."

"Very expensive." He kissed her again.

"It's just . . . just . . . that I wanted to live here. I like the town."

"Great place. You'll never regret it." This time he kissed her so she couldn't say anything more.

A cheer went up. She met his eyes and smiled.

"What time do you get off?" he asked.

"Why?"

"I'm taking you out. I'm sure Marie will babysit."

She wrapped her arms around his neck. "Fine, but tonight . . . let's take Cassie with us."

door closer
Lockset

Epilogue

Two years later

JAKE RACED IN THE DOOR. CASSIE SAT AT THE KITCHEN island, and Maggie was holding bobby pins in her mouth as she pinned Cassie's hair up in some fancy-looking style. Jake removed the bobby pins and kissed his wife's lips. She smiled and held out her hand, and he handed her one pin at a time until the hair was done.

He kissed Cassie on the cheek. "You look gorgeous."

He then crouched down in front of the twins, who sat in their bouncy seats on the floor. Russ shook his rattle, and Ray gummed his. Downy red hair was beginning to appear on their bald heads. "How are you two doing?"

Grins. Tiny hands, little feet in booties—he'd missed this stage with Cassie and was blown away by how quickly his boys were growing and changing each day. They'd be five months old next week, and Jake wanted to savor every moment.

"I laid out your suit," Maggie said.

Jake stepped over toys and baby items as he headed to the bedroom. He put on the suit and the tie, looked in the mirror, and gave his hair a quick run-through with his fingers.

He heard Marie arrive and say, "Cassie, don't you look pretty in that dress."

When Jake stepped out, Marie had Russ in her arms and was using one foot to rock Ray's bouncy chair.

"I pumped some milk. It's in the fridge," Maggie said. "They should nod off around seven." She glanced at the clock. "We've got to go. Thanks, Marie."

At the church, Jake made his way to the front beside Mark, Mark's son Andrew, and Gabriela's son Alfonso.

The organist began to play. Cassie walked up the aisle, throwing rose petals, followed by Gabriela's daughter, Carmela, and Gabriela's sister, Josefina. Gabriela came toward them in a long white dress, her hair up, her cheeks flushed, and her eyes sparkling. Jake glanced at Mark, who looked spellbound.

Father Norman smiled. "Friends, we are gathered here today to join together this man and this woman in holy matrimony . . ."

Jake met Maggie's smiling eyes, and something opened up inside his chest. It flowed like a river, exhilarating, deep, and satisfying. He fiddled with the knot of the unfamiliar tie, and Maggie tilted her head. Jake smiled and winked. He was undoubtedly the happiest man on the face of the earth.

Well, at least *one* of the happiest men, he thought, as Mark took his vows and began to cry.

天津滨海图书馆 «The Eye»
vocational college. Library
滨海区崇德道

Mount Pilatus, near Lucerne. Zurich

50 × 30H × 10 cm
(80+80) 张 20cm H

2015.
Feb. 20. 川页z东方
Toast master
London Cobble Museum 演出.

Dec. Barcelona Spain

2013.
Oct 群龙追台演奏.
Mench 30 ~ Apr 28 爸z蒙往思召.

2014. Berlin Wien
  Jul 泼克 Seattle.
  Sep. 群龙台演奏.

CPSIA information can be obtained
at www.ICGtesting.com
Printed in the USA
LVOW07s1934011217
558236LV00001B/3/P